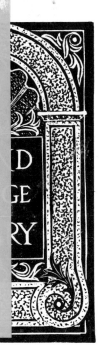

BROTHER
DUSTY-FEET

ROSEMARY SUTCLIFF

Illustrated by
C. WALTER HODGES

London
OXFORD UNIVERSITY
PRESS

Oxford University Press, Amen House, London E.C.4

GLASGOW NEW YORK TORONTO MELBOURNE WELLINGTON
BOMBAY CALCUTTA MADRAS KARACHI KUALA LUMPUR
CAPE TOWN IBADAN NAIROBI ACCRA

First published 1952
Reprinted 1961

Rosemary Sutcliff has also written

THE CHRONICLES OF ROBIN HOOD

THE QUEEN ELIZABETH STORY

THE ARMOURER'S HOUSE

OUTCAST

THE EAGLE OF THE NINTH

THE SHIELD RING

THE SILVER BRANCH

WARRIOR SCARLET

KNIGHT'S FEE

THE LANTERN BEARERS

Printed in Great Britain by Richard Clay and Company, Ltd.,
Bungay, Suffolk

Contents

Illustrations

I

THREE ADVENTURERS SET OUT

THE moment before it happened, Argos had been following obediently at Hugh Copplestone's heels; but then he saw the new ducklings. Golden, cheeping ducklings, scurrying all about the yard, while their comfortable brown hen-mother took a dust-bath in the corner by the big shippon. Argos was very nearly a deerhound, only his brindled black-and-amber coat was long and silky like a collie's. He had wallflower-brown eyes and a warm heart, and he loved all small scurrying things. So the moment he saw the ducklings he ambled over to blow at them affectionately; but the ducklings did not understand that it was affection, and they were very frightened. Hugh, who was on his way to water the calves, was carrying two pails on a yoke much too big for him, and did not notice what was happening until the ducklings scattered in all directions, cheeping and diving under anything that looked as if it might give them shelter from the Dreadful Monster, and the hen arose from her dust-bath with a wild squawk and flew clucking at the top of her voice to defend her adopted family.

'Argos!' cried Hugh frantically, setting down the pails with a clatter. 'Argos! Come *here*! Oh, hen, *do* stop making that noise!'

But it was too late. A window under the farmhouse eaves was flung open, and a scolding voice

shrilled down at him. ' Take that brute into the
cart-shed and tie him up. *I* saw him trying to kill
the ducklings, and a poultry-killer in this farm is a
thing I will *not* have ! '

' Oh, he wasn't. Really he wasn't, Aunt Alison ! '
protested Hugh, gazing up at her beseechingly.
' He likes ducklings; it was only that they didn't
understand.'

' Likes ducklings ! I don't doubt he likes ducklings ! ' snapped Aunt Alison. ' You take that
brute into the cart-shed, and I'll come and attend
to him later. Yiss ! ' And her head disappeared
and the window banged shut.

Hugh knew what she meant by ' attending ' to
Argos, and so did Argos, and his ears and tail
drooped miserably as he turned to follow his
master.

The cart-shed was dim and quiet, full of shadows
through which the May-time sunshine slanted down
like a golden sword from a hole high up in the wall.
There was no cart there now, because Uncle Jacob
had taken it to help a friend who was moving farms
—just the empty dimness and the golden sword of
sunshine. Hugh tied Argos up to a ring in the
wall with a piece of wagon rope; then he sat
down on his heels and put his arms round the
dog's soft neck, and held him tight; tight, as
though he was desperately afraid they might be
parted.

' Oh, Argos,' he whispered, ' you must learn not
to do things like that. Now she's going to beat you
again.'

Argos turned his head as well as he could and
kissed his master's chin with a warm, loving

tongue. He knew he was going to be beaten again, but he had been beaten so often that he was quite used to it, and Aunt Alison's shrill voice hurt him much more than the whiplash; and he tried to explain this to Hugh. But Hugh would not be comforted, and only hugged him the closer, while one tear trickled down his nose.

Hugh's mother had died when he was so little that he could not remember her at all, though his father had often and often told him about her, and how kind she was, and how she loved flowers, especially periwinkle. Hugh's father had been Vicar of a small, bleak Cornish village, and they had been very poor; but they had been very comfortable, and happy too, with a plot of periwinkle in the garden and an old woman called Hepzibah who came in by the day to look after them. But when Hugh was eight years old his father had died too, and he had had to come and live with Uncle Jacob, who was his mother's brother (though it was hard to believe that, because he was so different), and Aunt Alison, who was Uncle Jacob's wife. And Argos, who was a puppy then, had come with him. Uncle Jacob would have been fairly kind to them if he dared, but Aunt Alison grudged them the space they slept in and the food they ate—though Hugh worked hard enough to earn it—and she was very unkind to them. And as Uncle Jacob always did what she wanted, because she made him so uncomfortable if he did not, he was unkind to them too. Hugh would not have minded so much for himself, but very soon after he came to live in the big farmhouse, Aunt Alison had discovered that she could hurt him more by beating Argos than she could by beating *him*; so she had beaten Argos very often ever since, even more often than she beat Hugh, that is. She was not a nice woman.

'I must go now,' whispered Hugh. 'I must go and finish watering the calves, or she'll be even more angry. Oh, if only it was just you and me alone to ourselves in all the world!' And he rubbed his face against Argos's neck, and got up. At the opening of the cart-shed he looked back, and saw the great dog sitting up and looking after him. 'Good night, old Argos,' he said, and Argos thumped his plumy tail on the ground and whined softly in his throat. It hurt Hugh dreadfully to leave him there, but he turned away at last and set off to water the calves before going in to his supper.

Aunt Alison was alone in the big farm kitchen when he went timidly in, for it was May Fair over at Torrington, and Jenny the farm maid and all the farm hands except old Ammiel the shepherd were out enjoying themselves. Aunt Alison had had to let them go and enjoy themselves because of what the village would say if she did not, otherwise she would not have dreamed of it. She was taking pies out of the bake-oven (she always baked when Jenny was out, because it made her feel ill-used, which was what she liked), and her face was very red, partly because of the oven and partly because she was in a bad temper.

'I suppose you've forgotten to water the calves,' she said accusingly.

Hugh said, 'No, Aunt Alison. I've just done it.'

'Have you tied up that brute of yours?'

Hugh nodded miserably; and Aunt Alison

ladled some broth from an iron crock into a bowl and pushed it across the table to him, with a hunch of bread.

' There's your supper,' she snapped, ' and 'tis little enough you do to earn it.'

' I do work hard, please, Aunt,' said Hugh.

But Aunt Alison put her hands on her hips and screwed up her face and said, ' Work? Aye, you work, because I see that you do. You wouldn't do a hand's turn else, I'll be bound—and me working my fingers to the bone while everyone goes gallivanting off enjoying themselves.'

Her voice grew shriller and more aggrieved every moment. ' Yiss, and I'll tell you another thing, my beauty—'tis a fine affair that your uncle and I should have to feed and clothe and shelter the likes of you, because that zany father of yours was so busy reading books he couldn't even provide for his own flesh and blood.'

Hugh pushed away his broth-bowl and stood up to her with his hands clenched and his face nearly as red as hers. ' Don't you *dare* say things like that about my father,' he said, almost choking in his fury. ' You're a beastly woman, and I hate you ! '

There was an awful silence.

Hugh had never spoken even a little bit rudely to Aunt Alison before, and he couldn't quite believe that he had done it now. And just for a moment Aunt Alison didn't seem to believe it either; then her eyes began to glitter like glass in her red face, and she said in a triumphant and spiteful rush, ' You wicked, ungrateful varmint ! I've fed and housed you *and* that dog of yours for close on three

years, and *this* is what I get for all my goodness.
Not that it isn't what I expected, for well I know
the wicked ways of the world, and thank Heaven
I can do my duty and look for no gratitude! Yiss,
but 'tisn't my duty to feed and shelter that dog, and
I'll not do it another day.'

Hugh gave a frightened gasp, and his sudden
bright rage went out as though somebody had
thrown cold water over it.

Aunt Alison heard the gasp, and her face had a
pleased sort of look. ' He's no good for the sheep,
and he eats more than either of the other dogs,'
she said. ' I'll have him knocked on the head
to-morrow. Yiss!'

' No!' cried Hugh. ' Oh no, Aunt Alison.
He'll learn to be a sheep-dog, really he will. I'll
teach him. *Please*——'

' If 'twasn't that all the men are out except
Ammiel, and him a soft-hearted zany, I'd have it
done to-night,' said Aunt Alison. Then she
stamped her foot and pointed to the stairs. ' Oh,
get along to bed; I'm sick of the sight of you.'

For a long moment Hugh stood quite still, staring
at her red, triumphant face, and feeling very sick.
Then he turned away without a word, and stumbled
off upstairs, up and up to his garret high under the
eaves. And there he flung himself down on the
bed, not crying—it was too bad for that—just
lying quite still with his head in his arms, while
something deep down inside him whispered over
and over again, ' Good-bye, old Argos, good-
bye.'

He lay there for a long time, so long that it grew
dusk all round him, and the dusk deepened to dark,

and a bright star hung low out of the sky beyond his little window. And then, quite suddenly, he knew what he must do; and it was so simple that he could not imagine why he had not thought of it before. He must take Argos away to-night! They would run away together, and make their fortunes; they would find some place where Aunt Alison could not reach them and they would be happy.

Hugh got up off the bed, and thought about making preparations; but really there were none to make. He had a spare pair of shoes and a good shirt for Sundays, but he did not like to take them, lest Aunt Alison should call it stealing; and that only left the pot of periwinkle on the window-sill. It was a little bit of the periwinkle patch at home, which he had brought with him when he came to live here, and so it was his, and he could take it with him, and nobody could call it stealing; but it did not need to be packed or got ready in any way. So he simply sat down on the rush stool under the window, and waited.

Aunt Alison had not yet come to bed in the room below, and the others were not home from the Fair; so Hugh knew that it would not be safe to start out for a long while yet, and while he waited he began to make plans. It was a very quiet night, with hardly a breath of wind stirring; only the owls cried softly in the dark woods along the valley, and somewhere a dog-fox barked in the distance, and somehow the quietness helped him with his planning.

Should he go back to Cornwall, to the little bleak village that had been home before his father died? No, the people there were all so poor that none of them would be able to give him work. Well, then, should he wait in Bideford till daylight came, and wander down along the Quay where the great ships lay, and try to get taken on as cabin-boy aboard one of them, and see the Glories of Cathay or sail the golden waters of the Spanish Main? They would probably take him, because he was nearly eleven and tall for his age; but they certainly would not take Argos, so that was no good either. Then he had a great and glorious idea that was just as simple as the first one had been. They would go to Oxford!

Hugh's father had often told him about Oxford, where he had been servitor to someone called Anthony Heritage, at Oriel College. Being a servitor meant living with a friend who was richer than yourself, and sharing his schooling and his food, and in return for that, cleaning his boots and his room and carrying his books for him. That was the way in which most people who had not much money went to Oxford—or to Cambridge, for that matter. Well, so Hugh's father had gone to Oxford, and he had meant that Hugh should go too. ' I don't quite know how we'll manage it,' he had said, looking slightly bothered, ' because we don't know anyone who wants a servitor; but we're sure to find a way somehow, when you are thirteen or so.' (People went to the Universities much younger in the days of Queen Elizabeth than they do now.) And he told Hugh about Anthony Heritage, who hated learning and was generally in trouble with the authorities; and about the Bocardo Prison, where evil-minded students who got into debt and pawned their friends' Sunday

jerkins were locked up, and had to be fed from outside, because Bocardo did not provide meals.
About the Crosse Inn, where strolling players
acted their plays from time to time; and about
the wonderful lectures of Master Thomas Bodley,
and about the glories of the New Learning.

You see, until Henry VII was King of England,
very few people except the clergy had any learning
at all, and what books there were, were mostly in
Latin, and people were not supposed to think much
for themselves, in case thinking made them stop
believing in the Saints and being good. But in
some countries, people were already beginning to
make new discoveries, and learn what they wanted
to learn, and think for themselves about the things
they learned and discovered. All this was called
the New Learning, and little by little it started to
spread into England, and the English people began
to study all sorts of exciting subjects, and to think
long thoughts for themselves. Books began to be
printed in English so that everyone could read
them, and other people began to learn Greek so
that they could read some of the most wonderful
books in the world, in the language in which they
were written. It was all a kind of great adventure,
like a voyage of discovery.

Hugh's father had told him all about that; and
he had told him, too, about the towers and spires
of Oxford rising from a golden haze on fine summer
mornings, with Magdalen Tower rising above them
all, so beautiful that it was like an archangel standing with folded wings to guard the way into the
City; and how the first time he ever saw Magdalen
Tower there was a rainbow touching its pinnacles.

B

He had told Hugh about that so many times that whenever he thought about Oxford—which was very often indeed—he saw Magdalen Tower standing a-tiptoe to join hands with the rainbow.

So he would walk towards Oxford, and perhaps good fortune would meet him on the road, and if it did not, surely when he got there he would find someone who wanted a boy to tend their garden or help them keep their shop; and perhaps as time went on he would be able to get a little learning too. It would not be the same as going to Oriel, as his father had done, but it would be much better than nothing; and anyway, he and Argos would be together, and Argos would be safe from Aunt Alison.

Presently, as he sat waiting, he heard the farm people come home from the Fair, and the men clattering away to their sleeping quarters above the stables, and Aunt Alison scolding somebody. Then Jenny the farm maid came upstairs to the little garret next to his, and soon after that Aunt Alison came up to bed too. Hugh sat quite still on his stool, shivering a little, but not with cold, for it was not at all a cold night, listening to Jenny moving about on the other side of his wall and Aunt Alison thumping to bed in a bad temper in the room below. Soon everything was quiet again, but still he waited. He must give them all time to be sound asleep before he risked creeping downstairs. The night seemed more silent than ever; even the fox had stopped barking; only the owls cried in the darkness. Then there began to be another sound that came and went, and came and went: a kind of drone with a whistle at the end of it. Aunt Alison was asleep and snoring.

Hugh took off his shoes and got up very quietly, collected the pot of periwinkle, and stole across to the door. The hinges were rusty and squeaked as the door moved, so that he had to open it very slowly, inch by inch, until it was wide enough for him to squeeze through, and when he let it go the latch fell with a little ill-natured clatter that seemed loud enough to wake even the farm hands over the stables. He waited for a moment, holding his breath, but it could not have been as loud as all that, because there was no sound from the next-door garret, and down below Aunt Alison went on snoring. So he slipped out into the main loft. He did not dare to close the door behind him, lest it should make another noise, but luckily there was no wind to make it slam, and so he left it as it was.

He had to make two journeys down the ladder, because in those days shoes had no laces, and so you could not hang them round your neck, and you cannot climb down a ladder with both hands full—at least, not if you have to be quiet. So he took his shoes down first, and then went back for the pot of periwinkle, and brought that down too. He crept past Aunt Alison's door with the back of his neck prickling, and on down the stairs. The stair-well was pitchy dark, and he was terrified all the way down that he would stumble and drop his shoes, or miscount and tread on the fourth stair from the bottom, which always creaked loudly if trodden on. Once Aunt Alison stopped snoring, and he froze like a little wild thing when it scents danger, waiting for the bedroom door to fly open and Aunt Alison to appear at the stairhead with a

rushlight in her hand and her eyes glittering and
her head tied up in the huge white coif she always
wore at night. But the door did not open, and the
snoring began again, and after a moment Hugh
crept on once more, down and down until he
arrived safely in the kitchen.

The fire had been banked for the night, and the
shutters were closed, so the kitchen was as black-
dark as the stairs had been, but Hugh found his
way to the door without falling over anything, and
lifted the heavy bar which Aunt Alison had put in
place because Uncle Jacob was not coming back
until to-morrow, and slipped out, closing the door
very gently after him. He was free!

But he had forgotten about the two sheep-dogs,
who were always loose at night, and the next moment
they came baying and snarling round the corner
of the house as though they meant to alarm the
whole parish and tear him to pieces! Hugh's inside gave a sickening lurch, and he wanted desperately to run, but that would be no good, because
they would give chase and make more noise than
ever. So he stood his ground and spoke to them
quietly, holding out his hands for them to smell
as they came up. 'It's only me, Ship; it's me,
Lusty, only me.' And the moment they heard his
voice they stopped barking, and sniffed at his fists
in a friendly way, wagging their tails. 'Go to
bed!' whispered Hugh; and they padded off obediently into the darkness. But their barking had
roused Aunt Alison, and the next instant her window
rattled open, and Hugh knew that she was leaning
out to find what the noise had been about. He
crouched in the thick shadow against the house

'*Confound those dogs!*'

(See p. 14)

wall, not daring to breathe, and with his heart thudding away right up in his throat, so loud that he was sure she must hear it. But after what seemed a long while, she said, 'Confound those dogs!' and shut the window with a cross little slam.

With a sob of relief, Hugh took a firmer hold on his shoes and the periwinkle pot and darted out from the wall into the shadow of the cow-byre. Past the barn he went, and reached the black opening of the cart-shed; and then came the next danger, for if Argos barked to greet him it would set the other dogs off again, and they would be caught, Argos would be knocked on the head, and there would be no going away together and being happy.

'Argos!' he whispered, 'Argos, it's me—be quiet! Quiet, boy!' and next instant, before Argos had time to make a sound, Hugh was sitting on his heels with his arms round the big dog's neck, while Argos whimpered softly and kissed his master's face from ear to ear with his warm, loving tongue. 'We're going away,' he told him, untying the wagon-rope in a frantic hurry. 'We're going to Oxford—just us two, and Aunt Alison won't be able to beat you any more.' He threw aside the wagon-rope, and got up. 'We're going now— come on! Quiet!—Quietly, boy!'

Argos gave a little joyful whine and a little joyful bounce, and Hugh picked up his belongings and they went out together; out from the sleeping farm-yard and across the home-meadow towards a gate that opened into the deep-rutted lane.

The grass was cold and dew-wet under Hugh's feet and Argos's paws, and the night was full of little wandering scents of hawthorn and wet bracken. Behind them the farm slept, and the village in the coomb slept too, and only Hugh and Argos and the stars seemed awake in all the world. It was rather a lonely feeling. Then they came to the gate, and Hugh climbed over, because that seemed easier than opening it, and Argos crawled underneath; and they sat down in the ditch together while Hugh put on his shoes. Then Hugh found he had been quite mistaken about the world being asleep; it was as wide awake as ever it could be! Out in the open meadow he had not noticed it, but here in the ditch he could not help noticing; there were little rustlings through the grass, and little scutterings among last year's leaves, and a swish of wings along the hedgerow, and countless busy sounds of countless comings and goings, where the small folk of the wild were busy about their own affairs. It was nice to feel that the world was awake, after all.

When Hugh had put on his shoes he climbed out of the ditch and set off down the lane, he and Argos and the pot of periwinkle.

So the three adventurers set out on their way to Oxford, walking through the night, with their hearts very high within them—Hugh because he was going to seek his fortune, Argos because he was following Hugh, and the periwinkle because a periwinkle's heart is always high; you only have to look at its joyous little blue flowers to know that.

II

THE JOYOUS COMPANY

IT was growing light as Hugh, with the periwinkle under one arm and Argos padding at his heels, came down into Bideford town and across the Long Bridge. It was market day, and presently the town would be full of farm-carts and farmers with their wives, and sheep and pigs and cattle; but now it was very quiet, and the only things that moved were the river flowing towards the estuary, and a few gulls among the topsail spars of the shipping in the Pool. The sky was streaked with flaming cloud-bars of gold and saffron that grew brighter every moment, and Hugh, looking up to them, knew that he must hurry—hurry—hurry, because any minute now his aunt would discover he had gone, and be looking for him.

You would think, from the way she talked, that Aunt Alison would be only too pleased to be rid of both Argos *and* Hugh; but Hugh had a very uncomfortable feeling that he did a lot of work that she would have to pay someone else to do, if he was not there; and besides, she would not like it to be known that he had run away, because of What People Would Say. Aunt Alison cared a great deal about What People Said. And that being so, he must hurry! He crossed the bridge and climbed the steep hill beyond, and finding a road at the top that seemed to lead more or less in the right direction, set out along it.

He had no idea of the way to Oxford, and he would not dare to ask anyone until he was much farther from Aunt Alison; but he did know that it was somewhere to the east, and he thought if he kept on walking eastward he could not go very far wrong. And after he had walked a long way, perhaps to-morrow, he would stop at a village and go to the parsonage house and ask his road of the parson, because a parson was sure to know the way to Oxford, even if he had only been to Cambridge himself.

The sun was up now, and it felt warm and friendly on Hugh's face as he walked, and there was a little wind smelling of rabbits for Argos to sniff at. The white, dusty road beckoned them on and on, and the hedges were thick with hawthorn; the larks sang so high overhead that Hugh could not see them, however hard he stared up into the blue, and all along the hedgerows chaffinch and wren and robin were attending to their families. The cows woke up in the fields, and presently a few people began to pass on their way to market, and said 'Fine morning, my dear,' to Hugh, because West-Country folk never pass you without speaking; but none of them knew him, and afterwards none of them particularly remembered having passed a boy and a big dog and a pot of periwinkle, which was just as well. A long-legged cart-horse foal with bright eyes and feathery tail came galloping across one meadow to stick its head through the gate and pass the time of day with Argos; and Argos was thrilled, because he quite understood that it was a baby, although it was bigger than he was. So he kissed the foal, and the foal kissed him, and it was quite a long time before Hugh could get him away. But he managed it at last, and they went on down the dusty road.

Hugh's legs were beginning to grow tired, and he was dreadfully hungry, but he was happier than he had been for three long years, and he was sure that he would get to Oxford somehow, and that when he got there everything would be all right, because everything always is all right at the Foot of the Rainbow.

Of course it would have been easier if he had had some money, even a very little money. Still, he would be sure to find people on the way who would let him chop wood or carry water or weed their gardens or mind their babies in exchange for a meal for him and Argos. Quite soon hay-harvest would begin, too, when farmers were always glad of help, and perhaps he would find a farmer who would take him on for a week or two, and pay him a silver shilling. You could do a lot with a shilling, when Queen Elizabeth held court in Whitehall Palace.

Hugh was just thinking this when he turned a corner and came upon a cottage with a tethered cow and a few scratching hens, and at the side, the gayest flower-patch imaginable, where already the York-and-Lancaster roses were budding. And before the door of the cottage stood a small grey donkey wearing a pair of great plaited rush panniers, and a little old woman with a face as red as Aunt Alison's, but in a much nicer way. She was surrounded by neatly plucked poultry, green cheeses and baskets of eggs and bunches of gay cottage flowers, which she was trying to pack into the panniers, while the small donkey *would* not stand still, but sidled about and flapped its ears in the most annoying fashion.

Hugh came to a halt when he saw this, and said, 'May I help you, mistress?' (And really he would have stopped even if he had known that the old woman would not give him anything to eat; but he did rather hope that she would.)

The little old woman looked him up and down, with her head on one side like a robin, and then she said, 'You'm hungry, I reckon?'

'Yes, mistress.'

'Well, if you'll hold on to Posy before her puts her gurt foot amongst the eggs, and keep her quiet while I packs the panniers for market and puts on my cloak, I'll give you what I can.'

So Hugh put down the periwinkle and told Argos to guard it, and went and hung on to Posy's head. Posy was a nice donkey, really, and when Hugh stroked her nose she stopped sidling about, and stood still, twiddling her long ears in a pleased sort of way; and quite soon the panniers were firmly packed, with the fowls and cheeses underneath and the eggs and flower-bunches on top.

'My Good Man's laid up with the rheumatics,' said the old woman, as she gave everything a final pat, 'and I n ever can manage Posy by meself; and well she knows it, the li'l madam! Now do 'ee keep her quiet till I come back; I won't be but a li'l while,' and she toddled off into the cottage.

Hugh went on stroking Posy's nose, and Argos sat bolt upright, with one eye on the periwinkle to see that it did not run away, and the other on Hugh because he loved him.

The old woman was gone much longer than a little while, but she came back at last, in a faded scarlet cloak, with a large straw hat tied on over her coif. In one hand she carried a thick wedge of dough cake with a lump of cream cheese on it, and in the other a very nice bacon bone. She gave the dough cake to Hugh, and she was just going to give the bone to Argos when Hugh said, ' If you please, mistress, I'll take it for now, and we'll both have our dinner a little later on.'

So she gave it to him, and then hoisted herself on to Posy's back behind the panniers, while he went on holding Posy's head for her (with the hand that was not full of dough cake and bacon bone). She was a very little old woman, but by the time she was settled, with her cloak tucked in round her, there was nothing of Posy to be seen but four round hooves and two long ears and a velvet muzzle.

Hugh gave Posy a final pat on her nose, and stepped back. ' Thank you very much for the food, mistress,' he said.

But instead of riding off, the old woman sat looking down at him from under her big straw hat. ' Where are you going, my dearie,' she asked, ' you and the big dog and the pot of periwinkle ? '

' We're going to Oxford,' said Hugh. He had not meant to tell anyone until he was many miles farther from Aunt Alison, but somehow he was sure that he could trust the little old woman. ' Do you know the way ? '

She shook her head. ' Not I, my dear.' Then she rummaged under her cloak and brought out something very small and bright. ' Here be a three-farthing bit to help you on your way. Silver's lucky on a journey; iss surely,' and she dropped it into Hugh's hand.

' Oh! ' said Hugh, ' Oh, *thank* you, mistress! It's —it's very kind of you.'

' Bless your heart; may your journey be happy,' said the old woman.

She nodded and smiled and shook the reins, and after a time Posy decided she might as well move. Hugh turned to watch them—the little donkey, and the little old woman in the scarlet cloak, and the big panniers on either side—until they turned the corner of the road. Then he put the three-farthing bit carefully into the pocket inside the breast of his doublet, and stowed the dough cake down his front, and picking up the periwinkle, started out again, carrying the bacon bone in his free hand. Argos, who had been watching that bone hopefully since it first came out of the cottage (though he would never have dreamed of touching it before Hugh said he might), walked on the side of Hugh that the bone was, so as to keep it under his eye.

They walked on for a long time, by spinneys and meadows and open moorland, carefully avoiding villages, until the time came when Hugh knew he could not go any farther until he had rested for a while, and he was so hungry that he felt rather ill. Then quite suddenly the road came out from the shadows of a little wood, and there was a small hump-backed bridge and a streamlet and a wide, green valley beyond. The stream had alder-fringed banks that looked very comfortable for sitting on, and the water that flashed and flickered

over its bed of speckled stones looked as though it
would be wonderfully cool and comforting to hot,
way-weary feet. So Hugh turned aside from the
road, and, following the stream a little way, sat
down and took the dough cake and cheese from
inside his doublet. If Argos had all the bone,
Hugh thought, it was quite fair that *he* should have
all the cheese. So he put the bone in front of
Argos and the cheese in front of himself, and divided
the dough cake carefully into two halves, putting
Argos's share with the bone.

' There,' he said, ' you can have it now.'

It did not take long to eat their dinner, and when
they had finished they picked out the crumbs from
among the grass-blades, because they were still
hungry. But Hugh kept one little bit of dough
cake from his share, and threw it away into the
long grass, and Argos did not go after it, because
he understood that it was the Good Piece—the
last scrap of every meal that must be left for the
Fairy Folk. Old Hepzibah, who had kept house
for Hugh and his father, had always put aside the
Good Piece, and she had taught Hugh to do the
same.

After that they had a long drink, and Hugh
took off his shoes and hose and washed his hot
tired feet in the clear cold water of the stream, and
looked at Argos's paws to see that they were not
getting sore. Then he made sure his precious
three-farthing bit was safe, and lay down flat on
his back.

It was lovely to lie staring up through the young
green of the alder leaves to the blue beyond, and
waggle one's wet toes in the sunshine. The turf

was soft to lie on, and the stream sang by, and the freckled leaf-shadows fluttered over his face; from the woods across the valley the year's first cuckoo called softly, and when presently Hugh rolled over on to his elbow he saw that the meadow was all aflitter with lady's smock. It must have been like that before he lay down, but he had been too tired and hungry to notice. Then he saw a V-shaped ripple travelling up-stream, which he thought must be an otter, and he lay for a long time watching for it to come again, but it didn't, and at last he began to think it was time they took to the road once more. He would have liked to go on lying on the sun-dappled bank and waggling his toes all day, but he was a long way from Oxford, and he could not be more than twenty miles from Aunt Alison; and so he sat up and began slowly to put on his shoes and stockings. His feet seemed to have grown a good deal too big for his heavy shoes, but he got them on at last, and stood up.

'Argos,' he said, 'we must be getting on, old lad.'

Argos, who was sleeping peacefully with the remains of his bone between his paws, opened one eye, and then shut it again, pretending he had not heard.

'We must go just a little farther before dark,' Hugh explained. 'Truly we must.'

So Argos got up, stretched first his front legs and then his back ones, and picking up the remains of the bone, looked about him in a bothered sort of way. Then he buried it very carefully among the roots of an alder tree, while Hugh waited; and they set out again, trudging wearily down the road.

But their legs were very tired, and dough cake
and cheese and bacon bone is not really a very
sustaining meal when you are walking all the way
to Oxford; and after they had crawled on a few
more hot and dusty miles, they found a nice dry
ditch and simply tumbled into it and lay down.
They were so weary that not even their hunger
could keep them awake, and long before the daylight faded they were sound asleep, cuddled together for warmth and company, Hugh with his
arms round Argos's neck, and Argos with his head
on Hugh's chest, and the periwinkle carefully
lodged in the crook of a tree-root farther up the
bank. The dimpsey came and then the dark, and
the stars peered down at them through the hazel
scrub and white-flowered lady's lace; the little
creatures of the wild came and looked at them, and
decided that they meant no harm, and went away
again. And Argos dreamed that he was chasing
dream-rabbits, and Hugh dreamed that he was
walking to Oxford under the sky-wide arch of the
brightest rainbow he had ever seen.

They slept late next morning, and Hugh woke to
find the sun poking golden fingers down at him
through the lady's lace and hazel leaves and wild
marjoram. For a little while he did not remember
how he came to be there, but just lay blinking
sleepily up at the brightness and thinking how pretty
the nut-leaves looked with a rim of greenery golden
light round each one. Then suddenly he remembered about Aunt Alison having meant to have
Argos knocked on the head, and how he and
Argos and the periwinkle had all run away together and were walking to Oxford. And he sat

up with such a jerk that the big dog, who was still bunched up on top of him, rolled over with a crash and woke up in a floundering sort of way. For a moment it was all arms and legs and paws and waving tail, and then Hugh and Argos disentangled themselves, and sat up in the ditch and looked at each other.

' We've overslept,' said Hugh.

' Yee-ow ! ' said Argos, leaping out of the ditch and stretching first his front legs and then his back ones, and yawning so wide that Hugh could see right down his pink throat.

Hugh made sure his three-farthing bit was safe, and collecting the pot of periwinkle, scrambled out too. Just at first he was so stiff all over and his feet hurt so much that he could hardly crawl along, but after a while the stiffness and soreness wore off a little. He was very hungry, too, but that did not wear off; it grew worse and worse as he trudged on down the road, until it became a dull gnawing pain in his inside. Still, he must be more than twenty miles from Aunt Alison, and Argos was safe, and at the next village they came to he meant to walk boldly in and find the parsonage and ask the way to Oxford. So when they came to a wayside pool he stopped to wash his face so that he should look tidy and respectable for the parson.

It was a very still, dark pool, rimmed round with brown-tufted rushes and water forget-me-nots, and when Hugh knelt down and bent over it, his own face looked up at him just as clearly as from a mirror; a thin, brown, dirty face, with a large curly mouth; not at all respectable. He washed

it very hard to see if that would improve it, and
then he washed his hands and had a drink (Argos
had already had one), and brushed himself down
as well as he could. Then he smoothed Argos's
beautiful brindled coat so that he should look his
best too, and gave the periwinkle a palm-full of
water. It already looked its best, and perfectly
tidy and respectable; periwinkles always do.
After that they went on again.

But before they came to a village they came to
an inn. A rather tumble-down hedge-tavern, with
a clump of crazy outbuildings beside it, and a great
bush of greenery on the end of a pole sticking out
above the door for a sign. And lounging at their
ease before it, with a large, black leather ale-jack
between them, were a little company of men.

The moment Hugh saw those men, he began to
walk slower, and slower still; and when he came
opposite to them he turned into a field-gate and
stood there, pretending to do something to his
shoe, and stealing shy glances at them every few
moments; and then he gave up pretending altogether, and simply stood and stared at the little
company before the inn. He knew that it was
rude to stare, but somehow he *could* not turn his
back on them and go on down the empty road.
It was like being cold, and suddenly coming to a
bright fire: you don't want to go on again and
leave all the warmth and light behind you.

There were five of the men, and they were ragged
and travel-stained and mostly rather dirty, but
every one of them had little gallant touches about
his tatterdemalion clothes. They had brighter
eyes and clearer voices than any Hugh had known

before; and altogether there was something about them that seemed to Hugh very joyous, as though they had more starshine in them than most people have.

One of them, a tall, dark, swashbuckling sort of person who seemed to be the leader, had an early rose stuck behind his ear. One was a square, merry-looking man with sparkling rings in his ears and a limp peacock's feather in his bonnet. Another, who had a melancholy expression and seemed very proud of his legs, had scarlet stockings, and rosettes (what people called 'provincial roses') of tarnished tinsel ribbon on his dusty shoes; and the fourth, who seemed only a few years older than Hugh, had gold cords looped round the crown of his battered beaver hat. But the fifth man was the most splendid of them all, and instead of rings in his ears or rosettes to his shoes, he had a little bright Spanish dagger in his belt. He was lean and brown, and lithe as a wild cat, with very long arms, and his curly dark head set deep between his shoulders. His face was long too, and thin, and rather sad despite its curling laughter lines. Somehow he made Hugh think of Rahere, the King's Jester, whom his father had told him about: Rahere who had founded Saint Bartholomew's Hospital in London and been the one person in England who was brave enough to tell Henry I when he ought to be ashamed of himself.

For a while the five went on talking among themselves and passing the ale-jack from hand to hand, without noticing Hugh at all; and then, chancing to swing round, the man with the rose behind his ear saw him.

'Hi! my young cockalorum! Will you know us again if you meet us?' called the man, grinning. 'Best pull those eyes of yours back into your head before they pop clean out!'

The others laughed, but the Fifth Man touched his shoulder and said something in a low voice, and then called to Hugh, 'Brother Dusty-Feet, come over here and join us.'

Hugh said no word. He took a firmer hold on the pot of periwinkle, which was growing very heavy, and crossed the road with Argos padding at his heels, and stood looking up at the man hopefully, while they stood and looked down at him—and at Argos—and at the periwinkle.

'Well,' said the leader, in a rich and friendly voice, 'have you never seen actors before, that you stand in gateways and stare, with your eyes growing more like gooseberries every moment, and your mouth gaping wide enough to catch a cuckoo in it?'

'No, sir,' said Hugh.

So that was what they were: Strolling Players!— People who wandered up and down the country acting their plays in inn-yards and at the foot of market crosses. He had heard of such people, of course, but never seen them; and now he realized what a lot he had missed in not knowing them before; and he thought how splendid it would be if they were going his way and would let him travel with them.

'If you don't mind,' he said, 'where are you going, please?'

'Anywhere—everywhere,' said the leader, with a superb flourish of his right arm. 'We come and

go like the wind. We follow the road to the Foot
of the Rainbow—but so far we have not found any
gold.'

When the leader spoke about the Foot of the
Rainbow, Hugh knew that he simply *must* go with
them, somehow, anyhow. They were the Fortune
he had been so sure would meet him on the Oxford
road, and he wanted to go with them more than
anything in the world. ' Please let me come with
you,' he begged in a desperate rush. ' Oh, *please*! '
and waited for their answer, gazing up at the Fifth
Man, while Argos wagged his tail beseechingly.

Just for a moment there was a surprised silence.
The Players looked at each other, and then at
Hugh, and then at each other again.

' He's rather small,' said Scarlet-Stockings, doubtfully.

' He'll grow,' said the Fifth Man, ' and we need
another boy. Nicky's getting too big to play girls'
parts much longer.'

' Take what fortune sends, *I* always say,' said the
man with the peacock's feather.

But the man with the rose behind his ear pulled
at his little pointed beard and said, ' Not so fast,
lads.' Then he looked Hugh up and down in a
considering way, and demanded, ' What might
your name be, Brother Dusty-Feet? '

' Hugh Copplestone, please, master.'

' Well, then, Hugh Copplestone, it is not the
custom of those who travel the roads to inquire
into the past history of any they may chance to
meet with on their—er—peregrinations. Indeed,
to do so is regarded among all true Dusty-Feet as—
er—a gross breach of etiquette. But if you will

pardon my saying so, you are a rather small vagabond, and you don't look as if you had been one
long. Would you by any chance be running away
from your kind home and grieving parents?'

Hugh took a deep breath and explained about
Aunt Alison meaning to have Argos knocked on the
head, and how they had run away together and
were travelling to Oxford to seek their fortunes.
When he had finished, there was another silence,
and Hugh was sickeningly afraid that they were
going to turn him away; so afraid that his mouth
went quite dry, and he could only stand and gaze
at them, with his face growing whiter and whiter
under the brown.

'Well,' said the leader at last, 'do we take him,
lads?'

'Yes,' said everybody, and 'might as well,' they
added.

'Of course we take him,' said the Fifth Man.

So the leader bowed low to Hugh, doffing his
bonnet with a flourish that was simply superb, and
laying his other hand upon his breast. 'Then,
Hugh Copplestone, I have the honour to inform
you that your fortune is as good as made! You
have fallen into the hands of those who are the
masters of their art, the—er—shining lights of their
glorious profession; and ere long, with due care
and attention, you shall be a master of it likewise!
Why, before you can turn round, you will find
yourself playing St Cecilia before Gloriana herself,
as she sits on her golden throne in Greenwich
Palace!'

The boy they called Nicky said admiringly,
'What a liar you are, Toby.'

'*Your fortune is as good as made !*'

(See p. 30)

And quite suddenly, what with hunger and bewilderment and relief—but mostly with hunger—
Hugh found that the world was spinning round him
in the most uncomfortable way. He swayed a little
on his feet, and smiled a sickly sort of smile, and the
Fifth Man, who had been looking at him closely,
put out a hand quickly to steady him, and said,
' You haven't had anything to eat lately, have you,
Brother Dusty-Feet?'

Hugh shook his head carefully, and found that
the world was not going round as fast as it had
been, which was a relief. ' Argos too. I've got a
three-farthing bit,' he mumbled.

' Don't you worry about that,' said the leader,
cheerfully. ' Jonathan, take the gentlemen in and
regale them on fatted calves, while we get loaded up
and bring Saffronilla round.'

So the Fifth Man marched Hugh, who was still a
little unsteady on his legs, into the dark inn parlour, where a round young woman like a ripe
pippin gave him a large plate of pink ham and
brown bread, while Argos had a bowl of the most
delicious-looking scraps all to himself on the floor,
and the periwinkle shared the window-sill with a
pot of marigolds that belonged there.

The Fifth Man sat quietly watching, while Hugh
ate until he began to be gloriously full and the
world was quite steady again; then he asked,
' Why were you going to Oxford, Brother Dusty-
Feet?'

And Hugh told him about the New Learning,
and Magdalen Tower, and all the things his father
had told *him*, which he hadn't spoken about to anyone since his father died.

And the Fifth Man listened to him, with his head a little bent as though he was very interested indeed. Then he said, 'We're not going to Oxford, you know.' Hugh shook his head and went on eating; and the Fifth Man said, 'And you mustn't believe what Toby says; we're not a Queen's Company. We're ordinary Strolling Players, acting our plays in inn-yards up and down the country; and when times are good we eat as much as we want, and when times are bad we go hungry and sleep in the ditch. Do you still want to come with us?'

Hugh looked up, and found the Fifth Man smiling at him so that all his thin face quirked upwards at the outer corners, in a winged sort of way; and all at once Hugh felt that he would follow the Fifth Man over the edge of the world. 'Yes!' said Hugh.

So when Hugh had finished the ham they went out together into the sunlight. And there before the door was a very small tilt-cart with the ends of several planks sticking out behind, and a dappled mare half asleep in the shafts. It was a nice tilt-cart, rather rickety, but bravely scarlet, picked out with yellow; and the green canvas tilt was patched with blue so bright and joyous that it looked as if it was a patch cut from the clear sky; and the mare's dappled coat shone with grooming, her mane was plaited with golden straws, and her horse-brasses that were shaped like roses and stars and crescent moons sparkled in the sunshine. The rest of the company were gathered round, pushing odds and ends into the back of the cart or talking to the mare.

'Ah!' said the man with the rose behind his

ear. 'The gentlemen have fed, and the road calls us. But stay! Before we set out, you'd best know who we all are, beginning with myself, Tobias Pennifeather, devotedly your servant, the leader of this band of brethren—romantic villainy is my line. Gentleman with the die-away expression and scarlet stockings, Jasper Nye, who plays the lead in all our pieces. This with the peacock's feather in his bonnet is Benjamin Bunsell; comic relief, the trusty henchman who falls over his own feet. This in the laced hat, Nicholas Bodkyn, our Heroine. Make a curtsey, Nicky,' and Nicholas Bodkyn spread his imaginary skirts and dropped a billowing curtsey. 'That's right,' said Master Pennifeather, approvingly. 'Lastly, at your elbow, Jonathan Whiteleafe, who plays the devil in scarlet tights, and is the best tumbler in the South Country, beside.'

Then everybody was crowding round Hugh, patting him on the back and telling him that he would soon get to know which of them was which, and belting Argos in the ribs in a friendly way; and in the middle of it all he felt a hand on his shoulder, and the Fifth Man, who was Jonathan Whiteleafe, said in his ear, 'I'd put the periwinkle in the back of the cart, if I were you. 'Twill be quite safe there.' So they went round to the back of the tilt-cart and found a nice secure place for the periwinkle between a pile of planks, which Jonathan said were part of the stage, and a battered hamper with purple and spangles showing through the gaps in the wickerwork, which he said was a costume basket. Immediately after that Master Pennifeather gave the order to start.

'For we must be in South Molton before noon if

we're to put on a performance this afternoon,' said Master Pennifeather. 'And if we don't put on a performance this afternoon, we can't sup to-night. So gid-up, Saffronilla, old girl.'

Nobody seemed to be at all worried about supper being so uncertain, because they were used to it. Saffronilla, who had been dozing gently where she stood, woke up and shook her head and lumbered forward; the yellow-and-scarlet wheels of the tilt-cart began to turn, squeaking blithely, and they were off. The Players trudged alongside, Master Pennifeather with a hand on Saffronilla's neck, whistling softly but very cheerfully to himself; and Jonathan and Hugh and Argos all dropped a little to the rear, beyond the soft white dust-cloud (somebody always had to walk behind the cart to pick up the things that fell out). The three of them were very well contented with each other's company.

'If you get tired, you can ride on the shafts, you know,' said Jonathan, looking down at Hugh after a while as they trudged along.

But Hugh had forgotten about being tired or footsore; he was too happy to bother about things like that. He was part of this lovely, joyous, disreputable company. Before him the tilt-cart lurched and rumbled, wobbled and squeaked along the deep-rutted road, the dust curling up in spirals round Saffronilla's hooves as she clip-clopped along, and the brasses on her collar and breast-band chiming and jingling like all the bells of Elfland. The hedges were clouded with lady's-lace and flushed with campion, and the cuckoos called from the woodlands far and wide; and it really seemed to Hugh that summer had come to the world overnight.

III

THE TRUE AND NOBLE HISTORY
OF ST GEORGE

THEY travelled rather slowly, because the
lanes were not really meant for carts, and
sometimes they were so narrow that the
wheels were in the ditch on both sides, and the
branches of hazel and beech and elder along the
crest of the hedges brushed the top of the tilt with
a noise like breaking seas. But they got through
even the narrowest places with a little care and
pushing, and it was not yet noon when the Company
came in sight of South Molton, and halted to sort
themselves out so as to make a proper entrance.
They unpacked from the tilt-cart a drum and a
strange and curly musical instrument called a
sackbut; and then they went on again, Master
Pennifeather with the drum and Benjamin Bunsell
with the sackbut marching ahead of Saffronilla,
Nicky Bodkyn and Jasper Nye marching on one
side of her, and Jonathan and Hugh and Argos
on the other. It was a lop-sided arrangement,
but that could not be helped.

'We shall have to train yon noble hound to walk
in front,' said Master Pennifeather. 'With Morris-
bells on his collar, the effect should be superb.
Completely superb!'

Hugh was not at all sure that Argos would take
to walking in front with Morris-bells on his collar,
but of course he did not say so.

So they marched into South Molton to the joyous music of drum and sackbut playing ' Crimson Velvet ', with their heads up and their legs straight, not at all in the comfortable way they had been trudging along the country lanes, and not at all as though their shoes were stuffed with rags because the soles were worn through. Saffronilla pricked up her ears too, and lifted her sleepy head and minced along like a fine lady; and even the tilt-cart pulled itself together and stopped dropping things out behind. It was a triumphal procession, and as it wound along the narrow street, heads poked out of windows under pointed eaves, and people came running to house doors and down alleyways to see it pass and throng round it and follow on behind. The shout went up that the Players were coming, and everybody seemed pleased to see them.

But through it all, the Players swaggered on with their noses in the air, taking no notice of the merry crowds, for they had found long ago that it did not pay to be too friendly at first, because if you were, people decided that you were only human like themselves, and did not come to see you act; and then you had no supper and probably had to sleep in a ditch as well. Across the Market Square they went, and in through the dark courtyard arch of the inn.

After that everything was rush and scurry for a while. First they got leave from Mine Host to perform in his inn-yard, and then Jonathan and Master Pennifeather went off to get a licence from the Mayor. (Strolling Players had to get a licence from the Mayor in every town where they wanted to perform their plays, or from the Justice of the

Peace if there wasn't a Mayor. It was a great nuisance, because sometimes the Mayor or Justice was away or ill or just plain bad-tempered and disobliging.)

Meanwhile the rest of the Company set to work to stable Saffronilla, and borrow empty barrels to support the stage, and unpack the costumes and properties. They were hard at it when Jonathan and Master Pennifeather came back with the licence and went off again with the drum and sackbut to cry it through the town that, at four o'clock that afternoon, they were going to enact the True and Noble History of St George. And Hugh was hard at it, too. Wide-eyed with interest and excitement, he staggered back and forth, helping to carry the heavy stage-planks for Nicky and Benjamin to set in place across the borrowed barrels, and watching the costume hampers unpacked and the glory of colour and sparkle that came out of them, and fetching and carrying for everybody. At first Argos helped him, but after a time everybody got so tired of finding Argos just behind them when they stepped back, and so exasperated when they fell over him or found him standing just where they wanted to put something down, that Hugh took him into the stable where they were to sleep (a stable is cheaper lodging than an inn-chamber) and sat him down beside the periwinkle and told him to guard it. When he got back into the courtyard again, Jonathan and Master Pennifeather had returned from telling the town about the afternoon's performance.

At last everything was ready, and the whole Company sat down on the edge of the horse-trough or the shafts of the tilt-cart and ate bread-and-cheese in a hurry; and Hugh had a chance to look about him and notice things for the first time. The inn courtyard was a nice place, with carved oaken galleries that ran all round its whitewashed walls, and its steep gabled roof had been newly thatched, and was golden as a honeycomb above its many little bright windows. Usually, Hugh thought, it must be rather a sleepy courtyard, but to-day it seemed wide awake and eager for the play to begin—almost as eager as Hugh himself, and that was very eager indeed, because he had never seen a play before, and had no idea what it would be like, except that it would be lovely. The stage had been set up at one end of the yard, sticking out into it, because in those days people sat round three sides of a play instead of only in front of it, as they do now; and its position had been carefully arranged so that the door of the little room where the Players were to change their clothes was just behind it. Hugh knew that was what the little room was for, because Nicky had told him, and besides, he had helped to carry in the costumes —a King's robe of French rose-scarlet velvet with most of the nap rubbed off, a Bishop's mitre, a yellow satin farthingale rich with tarnished spangles, and a wonderful green paste-board dragon's head, and a great many other things of the same sort. There was nothing on the stage as yet, but somehow that made it all the more exciting, because you felt that at any moment the emptiness might become a trackless forest or a King's palace or the deck of a ship under full sail.

But Hugh was not left long to look about him,

for the moment all the bread-and-cheese was gone,
Master Pennifeather said it was time to be changing.
'Our new brother will learn best by watching, for
the first day,' said Master Pennifeather. 'Take
him up to the gallery, Jonathan, before the townsfolk begin to arrive.'

So Hugh and Jonathan, and Argos, who had
been brought from guarding the periwinkle because
they thought it would be good for him to get used
to crowds, all went up the steep stairway to the
gallery. Along one side of this gallery were the
doors of the bed-chambers, and along the other side
was the carved balustrade that kept people from
falling on their heads into the courtyard.

Jonathan planted Hugh and Argos against the
balustrade where it curved out above the inn door,
saying, 'You can see beautifully from here. Hold
on, and don't move when the folk start arriving, or
you'll get lost in the crowd.'

And with a nod, he set one hand on the rail and
vaulted over into the yard below. He halted an
instant to look up at Hugh, with his thin face
quirking up towards his ears, and then went swinging across the yard to the little dark doorway
behind the stage, where the others had already
disappeared.

Almost at once people began to arrive to see the
play. Prentice lads in flat caps, and farm lads
with leggings of plaited straw, and servant maids
in striped calico petticoats, farmers and master-
craftsmen with their wives and daughters, trooping
in through the dark archway, in ones and twos and
little merry groups, all happy and excited at the
unexpected treat, and many of them in their

Sunday clothes, with washed faces and knots of
ribbon on their sleeves, so as not to be out-shone by
their neighbours. More and more people, laughing and pushing and jostling their way in, packing
closer and closer into the courtyard and flowing up
the stairs to the gallery, until Hugh and Argos
could not have moved if they had wanted to.

Then Jonathan appeared again, with a long
trumpet that flashed golden in the sunshine, and,
springing on to the stage, sounded a loud, lovely fanfare that seemed to Hugh to flash golden too. Instantly the laughing and shouting and pushing
stopped, and everyone looked at Jonathan, standing alone above them, with his shabby doublet
seeming as gay as any jester's motley. There was
a hushed, breathless waiting moment after the last
notes of the fanfare had died away, and then
Jonathan made a low, swashbuckling bow to the
audience, and sprang down from the stage—and
the play began!

There was hardly any scenery; just a couple of
stools and a lot of labels. That was how it always
was with strolling companies in those days. It is
wonderful what you can do with a stool, especially
if you put a label on to say what it is meant to be:
spread a scrap of crimson damask on it, and it is a
King's throne; tie a green branch to it, and it is a
forest tree—if the label says so. Hugh could read,
because his father had taught him, and a few of
people in the crowd could read too, and told the
ones who couldn't, what the labels said. But
somehow, after a very short while, nobody would
have noticed if the labels were not there at all, for
the Players were making them see whatever they

wanted them to see, and the bare stage became
a woodland glade or a King's hall at a gesture
or a word. It is always like that with really good
actors.

To Hugh it seemed like magic. Of course he
knew the story of St George perfectly well, but that
did not make it any the less exciting, and he hung
forward over the carved balustrade open-mouthed,
wide-eyed and breathless, as the story was un-
folded on the little jewel-bright stage. He saw the
King of Egypt, in scarlet robes and a golden crown,
discussing with his bishop the dreadful dragon that
was living on his borders and having to be fed on
fair young maidens every day; and he saw the
King's daughter, exquisitely beautiful in a yellow
satin farthingale, led out by a sorrowing populace
and bound to a tree hard by the dragon's lair,
because she had drawn the fatal number for that
day, out of a hat (Benjamin's hat with the peacock
feather). Then, with a flash and a strong smell of
brimstone, the dragon leapt upon the stage and
opened its horrid red mouth and lashed its scaly
green tail. But just as it was about to seize the
shrieking Princess, up on to the stage sprang St
George, who waited only to explain to the audience
that he had been returning from a crusade when
he heard the screams of a maiden in distress, before
rushing upon the dragon with his sword gleaming in
his hand.

For one instant there was not a sound in all the
inn-yard, and then a tremendous uproar broke out.
People shouted for St George—'St George for
Merry England!' they yelled. 'St George!' while
a few of the prentices cheered on the dragon be-

cause they liked him best; and in the midst and
heat of all the turmoil St George and the dragon
were locked together in the most terrific struggle;
and hanging over the balustrade of the crowded
gallery, Hugh yelled and waved his arms, while
Argos stuck his head between the uprights and
gave little shrill puppy-yelps.

But at last the fight was finished, and the dragon
sank expiring on the stage, while St George stood
over him with sword up-raised, and everybody
roared louder than ever. Then St George freed
the Princess and took her home to her sorrowing
father, while the dragon crawled off the stage;
and after everyone had made long speeches, the
Bishop married them, amid general rejoicing.

Then the whole Company lined up on the stage
to bow politely, including the dragon, who had
taken off his paste-board head, so that Hugh saw
it was Jonathan.

So the Company bowed, and the audience
cheered; and then it was all over, and St George
had come down from the stage and was taking
round the hat (still Benjamin's hat). You see, in
those days you couldn't sell tickets as people came
in to see the play—there were too many doors into
an inn-yard, for one thing—you had simply to take
the hat round afterwards and hope that people
would put something into it. Some people did
not, of course, but most people did.

Little by little folk were making their way down
from the gallery and out of the yard, through the
archway into the Market Square, with or without
paying; and Hugh grabbed Argos by the collar
and flung himself into the crowd, darting and

swerving, diving and pushing and butting, first to the left and then to the right, down the stairway and across the courtyard to join his friends in the little room behind the stage.

Master Pennifeather was struggling out of the King's scarlet robes when he arrived, and Benjamin was taking off the Bishop's mitre, while Jonathan, still half inside the Dragon's skin, was helping Nicky out of the Princess's yellow farthingale.

'Well?' they asked. 'Did you like it?'

'Yes!' said Hugh. 'Oh yes, I *did*.'

'Come and take my crown, there's a good lad,' said Master Pennifeather.

They were nearly back in doublet and hose by the time Jasper Nye returned with the hat; and everybody hailed him eagerly. 'What luck, Jasper?' except Benjamin, who said, 'Oh, my poor hat!'

Jasper gave the hat to Master Pennifeather, who tipped the coins out of it on to the box they had been using for a table, and handed it to Benjamin. The silver and coppers rolled and clattered over the box top, and everybody gathered round to look, Ben Bunsell gently smoothing the long peacock's feather in his hat, which had got a little battered.

'By the fuss you make every time it's *your* hat's turn t'be sent round, anybody'd think 'twas a good hat,' complained Jasper, who always seemed too weary to talk properly when off the stage, and he laid down St George's breastplate and began to put on his doublet.

But Benjamin only grinned and shook his head, saying, 'Well, it *was* a good hat once, a very good hat, and I'm fond of it. There's no friend like an old friend, *I* always say.'

And all the time, Master Pennifeather was counting out the coins into the different piles; so much to settle the inn's bill next morning, so much against a rainy day or the price of new costumes, and a third pile to be divided amongst the Company.

'This is what we Players call the "sharing table", Brother Dusty-Feet,' Jonathan explained, as Master Pennifeather began to divide up the third pile.

Sometimes there was no third pile, and little enough in the other two, but to-day there was silver for everybody, even for Hugh! Hugh had not for an instant expected that there would be anything for him, and when the small pile of silver pence and three-farthing bits was put into his hand, he could only stare from it to the Players and back again. 'Is it—is it really for me?'

'Course it's for you,' said Nicky, kindly but scornful.

'You're very g-good to me,' said Hugh, turning bright pink. 'But I've not earned it.'

'A pish and a flim-flam!' said Master Pennifeather, sweeping the money for their bill into a leather pouch. 'You helped us right nobly with the stage and costumes, and you're one of the Company now. Besides, you've brought us good fortune! We've not had such an audience for weeks, and we were down to our last shilling. Now we shall sup most royally.' He jingled the bag joyously. 'Ye saints and sinners! *How* we shall sup! No rehearsing to-night, lads! Clear all this away, and we'll spend a merry evening.'

So once again everyone went to work. The stage was taken down and the wicker costume baskets were repacked and dumped in the stable, ready to go into the tilt-cart in the morning; and in a wonderfully short time the Company were trooping in through the house-door of the inn, with money jingling in their ragged pockets and the glorious smell of roasting mutton to meet them on the door-sill.

Later that evening they were lounging at their ease around the blazing fire of beech logs in the long, black-beamed common room of the inn, with Argos sprawling in their midst, his front to the blaze and his flanks rising and falling contentedly as he slept. Hugh squatted on the rush-strewn floor, with Jonathan's knees to lean against. He was quite full of mutton and apple-pasty, rather sleepy, and very happy. It was so lovely to have a pair of friendly knees to lean against if he felt like leaning, and friendly faces to look up at in the fire-glow.

There were a lot of townsfolk in the long room, drinking their cider and making a great deal of cheerful noise, and in between while gaping at the Players, and pointing them out to new-comers. But the Players took no notice of them; they were used to being stared at and pointed out to people; besides, it was good for trade. They were talking idly of their plans for the summer, and of Stourbridge Fair, where they would meet old friends at the summer's end; and Hugh blinked at the fluttering green and saffron flames, and listened happily to all they talked about.

Presently Master Pennifeather said, ' You'll have

to write us another play, Jonathan lad, and alter the old ones so as to bring in a part for Hugh.'

Hugh screwed round to look up at Jonathan. ' Do *you* write the plays? ' he asked.

Jonathan laughed and shook his head. ' Not really.'

And Jasper Nye explained: ' Johnnie writes us a play sometimes, but for the most part we act th' old Miracle plays—nobody knows who wrote them. An' he alters 'em where needful, so's never t'have more'n five people on th' stage t'once.'

' There is no getting away from the fact, my lords and gentles,' said Master Pennifeather, ' that a company of five is a trifle small. We shall make our fortunes now that there are six of us! '

Everybody laughed because they knew that they would never make their fortunes, and they didn't care, and Ben Bunsell suggested, ' Seven, if you count Argos here. Why don't you put a faithful hound in your next play, Johnnie?—or a ravening wolf?—I swear we could teach him to play either part.'

Argos opened one eye, because he knew that they were talking about him, and wagged his tail, because he knew that they were talking kindly; and everybody laughed again, because he looked so very unlike a ravening wolf.

' Don't forget the pot of periwinkle,' said Nicky, who was sitting on the floor too, with his arms round his updrawn knees. ' Write a part for the periwinkle, Johnnie! ' and he grinned and poked Hugh in the ribs, to show that it was friendly meant.

Jonathan Whiteleafe said, ' I will write a play

with a part in it for Hugh, and a part for Argos, and a part for the periwinkle, and it will make our fortunes, and we shall ride about the country in a golden coach, and have a supper like the one we have just eaten, every night, and Ben shall have a new peacock's feather for his bonnet. And now I think it's time that Hugh settled in for the night. He's had a hard day.'

So Hugh got up, and Argos sighed and got up too, shaking himself and yawning.

'Good night,' said everyone. 'Good night, Hugh. Good night, Dusty.'

And Jonathan got up also, saying that he must go and mend his dragon's skin, which he had split across the shoulders. So he and Hugh went out together; out from the noise and crowd and laughter of the inn, and across the quiet courtyard to the stables, with Argos padding at their heels, and a horn lantern to guide them, for it was quite dark by now.

The air smelled cool and fresh, and the stars shone above the black gables of the inn; and inside the stable, when they reached it, the lantern-light fell golden on the straw, and Saffronilla whinnied to them softly from her stall at the far end. They went to her and gave her bits of bread which Jonathan produced for her out of the breast of his doublet, and rubbed her nose and made small soft good-night talk to her. Saffronilla's muzzle was like velvet, and her eyes were big and dark under the bloom of light that the stable lantern threw over them. She nuzzled first at Jonathan's hand, then at Hugh's shoulder, and then dropped her head to talk to Argos.

They left the two of them to make friends, and
went back to their own bit of the stable, where the
battered costume baskets were stacked, and golden
straw was piled high for bedding; and Hugh
stripped off his doublet and his shoes, and
burrowed in among the straw, thinking what a
lot had happened since he woke up in the ditch
that morning. Jonathan hung the stable lantern
from a hook in one of the low black rafters, and
sat down cross-legged with the dragon's skin across
his knees.

In a little while Argos came from talking to
Saffronilla and cuddled in beside Hugh; and Hugh
put his arms round Argos's neck, and they wriggled
and squirmed and burrowed until neither of them
knew how it was possible for anyone to be more
comfortable than they were. Then they heaved
two contented sighs, and lay quiet.

If Hugh turned his head very slightly, he could
see his pot of periwinkle, with its blue flowers
looking almost purple in the lantern-light, and a
star looking in over the half-door, and Jonathan
sitting cross-legged in the golden straw, mending
the split in his dragon's skin.

It was lovely to lie there, with Argos beside him
warm and furry and safe from Aunt Alison, and
watch Jonathan stitch—stitch—stitching away.

Jonathan seemed to understand that when you
are feeling particularly wide awake you can't go
to sleep just because someone tells you to; so when
he saw Hugh's wide, bright eyes fixed on him, he
said nothing about shutting them, but began instead to talk very quietly in his deep, beautiful
voice, stitching all the time. He told Hugh about

the Players, and about the roads they travelled and the towns they passed through, and about the queer and funny and exciting things that happened to them, and the folk they met with on their travels. Pedlars and acrobats and wandering ballad-sellers, performing bears and other companies of Strolling Players, and quack doctors who sold the Elixir of Life at fourpence a bottle. Crazy wandering beggars, too, who were called 'Tom-o'-Bedlams' and had drinking-horns and badges and signs and pass-words among themselves, so that they were really a kind of Secret Society. All the folk who came and went along the roads of green England, and were called Dusty-Feet—or sometimes, rogues and vagabonds—by the respectable folk who lived in houses.

After a while he began to tell Hugh about the plays they acted: the True and Noble History of St George one day, and the Martyrdom of St Sebastian the next, some play of Jonathan's own on the third and a Shepherds' Play at Christmas; and they all sounded lovely to Hugh.

'Is it nice, making plays?' he asked.

'Sometimes,' said Jonathan.

'I suppose it's very difficult?'

'Not my sort of plays, Brother Dusty-Feet; I can make up rhyming jingle standing on my head— quite literally.'

'Would it be harder to make—the other sort?'

'I don't know,' said Jonathan. 'I've never made the other sort, you see.' And there was a kind of ache in his voice that made Hugh want to say something comforting.

So he said, 'But you're a very good tumbler

anyhow, aren't you, Jonathan? Master Pennifeather said so.'

And Jonathan laughed softly and joyously, and
said, with the ache quite gone from his voice:
' I'm the best tumbler in the South Country; and
that's something worth being, after all.'

He knotted off his thread, and folded up the
dragon's skin and laid it on the top of a costume
basket. And Hugh suddenly found he was very
sleepy; so he shut his eyes and snuggled closer to
Argos, and long before the others arrived he was
asleep in the golden straw.

IV

THE PIPER

ALL through the first weeks of summer the little Company wandered east and northward, acting their plays in inn-yards and at the foot of market crosses as they went. They skirted the bleak slopes of Exmoor and strolled on to Taunton; they followed the coast to Bristol town, where the tall ships lay, and made their way up through the rolling Cotswold country until they came to the grey city of Gloucester and saw the pinnacles of the Cathedral tower reaching up as though to prick the evening sky and make more stars in it, and heard Great Peter among the bells that rang for Evensong.

Hugh had been with the Company for nearly two months now, and it was high summer; the hedgerows were all a-chime with foxglove bells, the beech woods layered with cool green shade where the midges bit you if you lay down for a rest, and the cuckoo's voice was breaking. Hugh had learned a great deal in those two months, and for quite a while he had been acting in the plays which Jonathan had re-written so as to make room for him. Everybody had a hand in teaching him to act, including Nicky, who said that the three things needful for playing women's parts were to be able to curtsey, screech, and manage your farthingale so that you did not fall over it. He taught Hugh to do all these things so well that by the time they reached Gloucester he could screech, as Master Pennifeather said, like a pea-hen, drop billowing curtsies that could not have been bettered by the stateliest of the Queen's Ladies, and sweep across the stage without once getting his farthingale mixed up with his own feet or anybody else's. Hugh generally played women's parts, for the women's parts were always played by boys in those days, so he found Nicky's lessons very useful indeed, though of course he learned a great many other things about acting too. Also he was learning to blow the long golden trumpet that told people when the play was about to start, because in such a little company, everybody had to be able to do everybody else's jobs; and he helped Jonathan to copy out parts, and altogether he was very busy. Argos was busy too, because he also was learning to be an actor; he had walked on as a Faithful Hound in several plays, and everybody said he was a very good actor indeed; and the pot of periwinkle was put on the stage to play the part of a garden or a Flowery Pleasance every time one was needed.

The whole Company were nice to Hugh in a rough-and-ready sort of way, and he was very happy with them, even when he was hungry. (They were all hungry between Taunton and Bristol, because the Somerset people did not seem to appreciate good acting.) There were the long marches, trudging beside the tilt-cart, the Company talking to Saffronilla or learning their parts as they went along; the heart-stirring excitement of each performance, with the stage set up in the heart of a crowded inn-yard, and hot supper and

warm straw for bedding at the long day's end, if
the audience had been good. And if the audience
had been bad, they tightened their belts for supper,
and slept in a convenient ditch or under a haystack,
and Ben Bunsell said, ' It's a long lane that has no
turning, that's what *I* always say,' which was
cheering, if not really helpful.

One lovely July morning the whole Company
were taking their ease on the topmost lift of the
Cotswolds. It was a baking hot day, and that was
why they had turned off the road for a rest, instead
of pushing straight on to Lillingfold Village, where
they planned to spend the night and play the
Martyrdom of St Edmund next day. The hill-top
turf was dry and warm to the touch, smelling of
thyme and little white honey-clover, and the
coloured counties lay spread below them, green and
grey, russet and purple, with here and there a
cloud-shadow that seemed to have a bloom on it
like the bloom on a sloe, drifting up from the south.
A little way off, Saffronilla cropped contentedly at
the wayside grass; and the little bronze grass-
hoppers chirred among the clover stems, and the
larks were tossing over the hills, filling all the blue
emptiness of the sky with their shimmering song.

Most of the Company were lying flat on their
backs; but Jonathan was propped on one elbow to
watch those cloud-shadows drifting across England before the warm south wind, and Hugh
sprawled on his front beside him. Hugh could
not lie on his back comfortably just then, because
last evening Master Pennifeather had beaten him
for getting too interested in the audience and forgetting about the part he was supposed to be play-

ing. Master Pennifeather had warned him before what would happen if he did it again, and so he had known what to expect, and there were no hard feelings on either side, but Hugh's shoulders were very sore. So he sprawled on his front beside Jonathan, and watched a small green beetle climbing industriously up and down its own little forest of thyme and clover stems. Argos was being a nuisance, because he was interested in the beetle too, and wanted to blow at it. The beetle did not seem to like being blown at by Argos, so Hugh had to hold his hairy face away with one hand all the time.

' Leave it *alone*, Argos! ' said Hugh. ' It doesn't like you.'

But Argos liked the beetle, and could not believe that it did not like *him*; and he went on blowing, so that at last Hugh rolled over and sat up, pulling Argos with him, and the beetle was left in peace.

' What is over there? ' asked Hugh after a little while. ' Way over there where everything goes flat and blue and misty and blends into the sky? '

' Oxfordshire is over there,' said Jonathan.

Hugh sat quite still, staring away and away into the blueness. Somewhere over there, then, would be the New Learning, and Magdalen Tower with its pinnacles touching the rainbow. It was funny to think that he had come so far on his way, and now he was not going to Oxford, after all—at least, not yet awhile. He still meant to go there one day. He thought about it rather dreamily, as people think of going to Samarkand or Hy-Brazil—or the Foot of the Rainbow; but he still meant to go, one day.

Then he chanced to look at the road, and as he looked, a strange figure appeared over the brow of the hill and came striding along it in their direction. He was a tatterdemalion creature; green and grey and russet rags fluttered about him, and he carried a long staff in his hand, and walked with a strange free lilt that made Hugh think of a wild animal.

'Look!' said Hugh. 'There's someone queer coming along the road. He's not a Tom-o'-Bedlam, is he?'

Everybody sat up and looked, and Jonathan said, 'No. I do believe it's a pilgrim of some sort. You don't see many of them nowadays.'

'And he's coming to join us,' said Master Pennifeather. 'We are honoured, my masters!'

The stranger had turned off the road and was coming across the turf; and as he drew nearer they saw that his skin was brown as a ripe hazel-nut, and his long hair as white as the seed-silk of the traveller's joy—though he did not seem old— and his eyes a strange dancing green. He had a leather scrip tied to his girdle, and a cockleshell in his broad-brimmed hat and a dried palm on his shoulder, and so many little bright pewter figures of saints fastened to his hat and his ragged cloak that he chimed and jingled faintly as he walked.

'Good-day to you,' he said, when he reached them. 'It is a very hot day; even the cloud-shadows seem half asleep in the heat. May I join you, here on this hill-top?'

'Join us and welcome,' said Master Pennifeather. 'Plenty of room for us all.'

And Ben Bunsell said comfortably, 'The more the merrier, *I* always say.'

The Palmer sat down between Hugh and Jonathan, and held out his hands to Argos; and, to Hugh's surprise, Argos thrust his muzzle into them, and thumped his tail on the turf and crawled closer until he could lay his head on the man's ragged knee.

'He's never done that before,' said Hugh, 'not to a stranger.'

'All dogs come to me,' said the Palmer. 'Creatures of the hearth and creatures of the wild, they all come to me.'

For a little while they sat there, the Players and the Palmer, not talking, just sitting in the sunshine in a companionable sort of way.

Presently Benjamin, by way of making polite conversation, said, 'You will have travelled a long way, friend, by the palm and cockleshell that you wear.' (For a cockleshell in a man's hat meant that he had made the pilgrimage to Compostella, and a palm at his shoulder meant that he had been to the Holy Land.)

'Aye,' said the Palmer. 'I have walked many roads and seen many lands and sailed many seas. I have seen Jerusalem from the Mount of Olives, as I came down the hill road from Bethany—that was in the spring, and all the upland pastures were scarlet with anemones, and the almond trees in flower. I have seen the Golden Gate, and I have sat me down on Mount Gilboa, as I sit now, and watched the cloud-shadows drift across the plain of Esdraelon far below, and all the plain was red; but where the clouds passed the red was changed to wine-purple. I have been to Rome and Compostella, and the golden city of Constantinople; and now I travel the roads of England from shrine to shrine, until the time comes when I go overseas again.'

He talked on for a while, of cities that had been great places of pilgrimage fifty years ago, and pilgrim tracks that were scarcely used nowadays. And Hugh wondered why he went on pilgrimages at all, now that so very few people did, until he noticed that the Palmer didn't seem to care much about the shrines, only about the roads that led to them. Then he understood that it was for the sake of following strange roads and always seeing over the top of the next hill, that the Palmer went on pilgrimages.

The Palmer said that he was on his way from Glastonbury to visit the shrine of Our Lady of Walsingham, and that presently, about Christmas time, he would go to Canterbury.

'Do you know the Palmer's way to Walsingham?' he asked. And when they said No, it was farther north than they ever went, he said, 'They grow saffron up there—whole fields of saffron like shining cloth-of-purple, and the road runs through them all the way.'

Then he picked up his staff and got up, just as suddenly as he had sat down; and one by one the Players got up too.

'We must take the road again,' said Master Pennifeather, stretching. 'Our ways lie together as far as Lillingfold. Will you keep company with us?'

The Palmer shook his head. 'I am for travelling

cross-country to-day. But lend me the boy until evening, and I will bring him back to you at Lillingfold.'

Master Pennifeather said, ' Should you like that, Brother Dusty?' (for somehow, Jonathan's name for him had stuck, though of course it really belonged to all wayfaring folk).

Hugh was surprised, because he didn't think the Palmer had noticed him particularly, and he was pleased because he wanted to hear more about distant lands; so he said, 'Yes! Yes, I would! Only I'll have to take Argos because I don't think he'll stay without me.'

So after they had arranged to meet at Lillingfold for supper, the Company split up, Saffronilla and the Players and the tilt-cart went off up the road, and the Palmer, with Hugh and Argos at his heels, went plunging away downhill.

The boy and the dog had to hurry—hurry—hurry, to keep up with the fantastic figure that went loping and lilting on before them, with rags aflutter in the south wind and the sunshine. From time to time he called to them over his shoulder, and from time to time he took a reed pipe from his belt, and, setting it to his lips, played shreds and snatches of country tunes that seemed to draw Hugh after him as though by a silver chain of sound; but always, after a few moments, he would put the pipe back in his belt.

On and on they went, the Palmer in front, the boy and the dog following enchanted at his heels; down from the stone-walled upland fields, and the sheep grazing on the thyme-scented turf, to the lush grass and the woodlands below. By deep meadows and reed-fringed streams and the green shade of beech woods they went, keeping always clear of the lanes and clustering villages where people might see them pass. Presently the Palmer slackened speed for the others to come up; and they went on three abreast, the Palmer in the middle, and Hugh and Argos on either side.

They went more slowly now, and the Palmer began to talk again, sometimes to Argos, but mostly to Hugh. But now, instead of pilgrim-ways and distant countries, he talked about the country they were passing through and the wild-lings that lived in it—strange talk, about the air-paths that the woodcock followed down from the north on winter nights, and the ways of the vixen with her cubs. He seemed to know as much about the green plover as though he had been one, and as much of Brock the Badger as though he had lived all his life in an underground sett. Many and many things he told Hugh: about dormice and curlews, wild bees and grass-snakes and otters; and Hugh jogged along at his side, forgetting his sore shoulders, and not even noticing how hot he was nor how tired his legs were getting.

At last, towards evening, they dropped into a wooded hollow with a speckled trout-stream sing-ing through its stillness, and all its slopes shadowy pink with foxgloves under the trees; and the Palmer suddenly grew silent and sat down with his back to an alder tree. Hugh sat down too, and watched him, hoping for more, and Argos settled himself at their feet. Presently the Palmer took out his reed pipe again, and began to finger it, smiling a little secret smile to himself all the while.

'Come closer,' he ordered suddenly. 'Come very close and sit very still, and you shall see what I never yet showed to anyone.' And he began to play.

It wasn't a tune exactly, not this time; it was just note after note, with now a pause, and now a run like falling water. And the woods grew very still to listen. Little shivers began to run from Argos's nose right down his back to the tip of his tail, and he crawled nearer and nearer to the Piper, until once again he dropped his head on to the man's ragged knee. Then a rabbit popped up from the undergrowth, hesitated, with twitching nose, and scuttled closer to sit on its haunches at the Piper's feet. Another came, and another; a russet field-mouse crept out from under the foxglove leaves, its eyes black as sloes and bright as stars in its tiny whiskered face. With a flash of living blue out of nowhere-in-particular, a kingfisher landed on a low branch beside the Piper's head. A robin came, and a hare, a bush-tailed squirrel, and a cock chaffinch with a breast as pink as a rose. The air was full of the flitter of soft wings, and the undergrowth was all a-rustle with bright-eyed furry creatures drawing in to the place where the Piper sat. They thronged round him, cuddling to his feet and perching on his shoulders, quite unafraid of Hugh or Argos. Hugh sat as still as the alder tree, and it seemed to him that the piping that had called Argos and the woodland creatures was calling him too, calling the heart out of his breast, reminding him of things he had forgotten quite soon after he was born, talking about the rainbow above Magdalen Tower, and all the dreams that he had ever dreamed in his eleven years. . . .

Hugh never noticed when the piping stopped; but suddenly he found that everything was quiet, and the long pipe was lying in the Piper's lap. Then, very slowly, the Piper held out his hands; and the wild things came to him as though by invitation. Soft little noses explored his finger-tips, long silky ears were laid back under his caressing hand; a mouse ran up his arm to his ragged shoulder, and sat there among the small birds, cleaning its face. . . .

At last the Piper dismissed them, with a slow, wide gesture of his hands, and once again the air was full of flittering wings, and there were whisper-ings and rustlings under the foxglove leaves; and when they died away, the little hollow was just as it had been before the Piper began to play.

The Piper looked at Hugh, with a smile glimmer-ing far back in his strange green eyes. 'A trick of the pipes,' he said. 'A fine trick, is it not?'

Hugh nodded. He could not speak just yet. He felt as though he had been somewhere a long way off, and had not yet quite got back. He was still a little dream-bound when he followed the Piper up through the freckled foxgloves to the meadow above.

'It is growing late,' said the Piper. 'See how the shadows reach out their hands towards to-morrow's dawn. We must be on our way.'

Once again he sped on in front, while Hugh and Argos followed at his heels; on and on, straight across country, as the rooks fly home at sunset, while the shadows lengthened and the evening grew more and more golden. At last they came through a spinney, and saw, farther up the valley,

The woods grew very still to listen

(See p. 61)

the huddled roofs of a village, with a church tower
rising in their midst. The daylight had scarcely
begun to fade, but already a candle shone in one of
the cottage windows, to welcome someone home.

' See,' said the Piper, halting on the woodshore—
and he put his hands on Hugh's shoulders and
looked deep down into his eyes, ' there is Lillingfold Village, and your friends are waiting for you.
But come away with me! Leave the light in the
window yonder, and come away with me to the
wildwood. I will teach you the magic of my
pipes; I will give you your forest heritage; only
come away with me now—now, before they come
to look for us.'

Just for a moment the pipes seemed to be calling
to Hugh again, but he shook his head and said:
' No, I'm sorry, but I must go back to my friends
now.'

' Perhaps one day, when you only see the stars
through a window-pane, and you've lost your
heritage, you'll wish you had come away with me
to-night.'

' I *don't* see the stars through a window-pane,'
said Hugh firmly. ' I'm one of the Dusty-Feet, like
my friends, and I'm sorry—I shan't ever forget
to-day—but I won't come with you.'

The Piper looked deep into his eyes for a moment
longer, and then he dropped his hands from Hugh's
shoulders. ' Aye well, go then,' he said. ' Go back
to your comrades.'

' Aren't you coming too?' asked Hugh. ' To
supper, you know?'

But the Piper said, ' No, I have bread of my own.
The joy of the wilderness go with you, small brown

brother.' And he turned on his heel and disappeared among the trees.

He had gone so swiftly and so silently that it was
as though he had simply melted into the wild that
he loved. Argos whimpered in a troubled way,
looking up into Hugh's face. Then they turned
back towards the village; and suddenly both of
them were very weary.

The shadows were rising knee-deep across the
meadows, but the sky was still full of sunshine, a
wonderful sky of golden green, barred with clouds
of fiery sunset that were like great wings. And
beside a little stream that ran between banks of
meadowsweet and rose willow-herb, they came upon
Jonathan, sitting peacefully with his back to an
alder tree.

'Hullo,' said Hugh, and sat down beside him.

'Hullo,' said Jonathan. 'Where's the Palmer?'

'He wouldn't come back to supper, after all.'

Jonathan nodded. 'And was it a good day?'

'Y-yes,' said Hugh. 'Yes, it was lovely. Queer,
too.'

'Queer?' asked Jonathan.

Hugh began to tell him about the queerness as
best he could; about the wonderful piping, and
the wild things that had come in answer to it, and
about the Piper wanting him to go away with him.
'Who—what do you suppose he was?' he asked,
when he had finished and Jonathan still sat gazing
in front of him. 'He wasn't an ordinary Palmer.
You don't suppose he was one of *Them*, do you?'

Jonathan looked down at him, smiling a little, so
that his brows and the corners of his mouth quirked
up towards his ears. 'Who knows?' he said. 'Call

him " the Piper " and leave it at that. It's not polite to ask too closely the Who and What of the people one meets on the road.'

For a little while they sat in a companionable silence, and then Jonathan uncurled his legs and got up. ' It's time we were getting back, or the others will have eaten all the supper.'

So Hugh got up, and Argos woke with a bounce and got up too, sneezing so that all his four legs shot in different directions; and they set off towards the village. By this time rushlights had been lit in other windows to welcome the menfolk home from work in the fields; and suddenly, just for a moment, they thought it would be rather nice to have a home; a home with a candle in its window.

On the outskirts of the village they met Nicky coming to look for them.

' We thought you'd all got lost,' said Nicky; and then he took a good look at Hugh, as well as he could in the dimpsey, and said, ' My eye! You look as if you'd been dragged through a gorsebush backwards! You haven't been pixie-led, have you, youngster? '

V

SEISIN

AFTER Lillingfold the Players turned south again, and for a little while, as the blue glimpse of Oxfordshire fell farther and farther behind them, Hugh felt as though something was pulling him the other way, reproaching him for turning his back on it, for breaking faith with his dream. But he wasn't breaking faith, not really, he thought; he still meant to go to Oxford—one day. And presently his regrets grew fainter and fainter still, until once again he almost forgot about it.

Through the rest of that summer they wandered on, by Malmesbury and Newbury to Maidenhead, where they acted a morality play on the steps of the Market Cross and Argos bit a fat Alderman who he thought was going to steal the tilt-cart. The Alderman kicked Argos, and the Players went to his rescue (Argos's, not the Alderman's), and there was a fight with the townsfolk, and they had to leave the town in a hurry to avoid being arrested by the Watch.

After that they headed for Cambridgeshire, and in the golden September weather all the world seemed to be heading in the same direction: merchants and drovers, other companies of players, pedlars and bear-wards, quack doctors and swarthy Egyptians, all pouring in to buy and sell, act plays or tell fortunes for pick-pockets at Stourbridge Fair.

At every corner they saw more people coming up the by-lanes; and when they were not passing slow flocks of sheep and droves of cattle, they were being passed themselves by rich merchants on fine horses with strings of laden pack-mules behind them. It was like that when they were still two days from the end of their journey, and by the time they came in sight of the fairground under the walls of Cambridge, the roads were so packed that they could hardly crawl along, and the dust rose so thick that everyone was powdered white with it, and their eyes got red and sore and it was hard to breathe without coughing.

Hugh had never seen a fair before, not even St Margaret's Fair at Bideford, because Aunt Alison had never given him a day off or a silver penny to go to it. So his first sight of the great Fair of Stourbridge left him dizzy and gasping. It was loud as a thunderstorm, glorious as a rainbow, and huge as the Four Cities of Fairyland rolled into one. But he did not get a chance to see much of it on the evening they arrived, because it was late and there was a great deal to do. They did not try to find lodgings at one of the inns of the city, because that would be much too expensive, and anyway, all the inns would be taken now, by bigger and richer companies; but after they had got the usual licence to perform, they went in search of a clear space that nobody else had found first, and when they found one, made camp on it. They tethered Saffronilla and fed and watered her, and proclaimed next day's performances, and then Jonathan spread his mat, and put on his spangled tights and tumbled for the little crowd they had just

gathered, until Jasper had collected the price of
supper in his hat.

But already old friends had begun to come across
each other, and Nicky, coming back with a pail of
water from the nearby stream, said, ' Zackary
Hawkins is here, but his man is laid up with boils
all over.'

' Ye saints and sinners! That's ill fortune!'
said Master Pennifeather. ' What does friend
Zackary mean to do about it?'

Nicky shrugged. ' Oh, carry on as usual and
risk it.'

And then, seeing Hugh's bewilderment, he explained that Zackary Hawkins was a quack doctor,
and that quack doctors were not allowed in the
great fairs because the real doctors had managed
to get a law passed forbidding them. So when they
did set up their stands at a fair they always had a
man whose job was to keep a look-out for the
stewards and law-officers, and give warning if any
came that way. Because Zackary Hawkins's man
was laid up with boils, he would have to risk being
taken unawares by the stewards of the Fair, which
was a nuisance.

' Oh, well, nothing venture, nothing gain, *I*
always say,' said Ben Bunsell, with his mouth full.
' Daresay we'll be able to do a bit of watch-dogging
for him, from time to time.'

When supper was over they lay down to sleep
under the tilt-cart, all but Jonathan, that is. He
sat up until midnight to see that nobody stole
Saffronilla or the costume baskets, and then he woke
Master Pennifeather to take his place, and just
before dawn Master Pennifeather woke Benjamin.

It would be like that all the time they stayed there, for a fair was not at all an honest place.

It was all so strange and exciting, that first night, that for a long time Hugh could not go to sleep at all. He lay listening to the night sounds of the great fairground and watching, between the spokes of the nearest wheel, the dark shape of Jonathan sitting beside the remains of the fire, until at last everything got blurred together and he was not sure which were camp-fires and which were stars. And then quite suddenly it was morning and the sun was slanting through the scarlet wheels of the tilt-cart, and the fairground was growing noisier every moment, as it awoke to the new day.

All that morning they were very busy putting up the stage and getting everything ready for the performance; and in the afternoon came the play itself, and a great crowd to watch it. And when the Players counted out the silver in Benjamin's hat on the sharing table, they found they were quite rich —rich enough even to spend a few pence at the sideshows if they felt like it, and *still* have enough to pay their Fair Dues when the time came for paying them.

It was quite early in the evening when the sharing-out was over, and so Jonathan, Nicky and Jasper, with Hugh holding firmly to a strap through Argos's collar, all set out to see the fun of the fair, while Ben Bunsell and Master Pennifeather stayed with Saffronilla and the tilt-cart on the understanding that it would be their turn next evening.

Before they set out, Jonathan said: ' Now, look here, Dusty; if you don't stick to the rest of us as close as a limpet, you'll get mislaid in five seconds in this crowd, and it won't be too easy to find you again.'

So Hugh stuck very close indeed, and before long he was in such a glorious maze and muddle, what with the noise and crowds and colour, the swirl and sweep and sparkle all around him, that he felt sure it would not take him anything like five seconds to get mislaid, if he once lost sight of Jonathan. They wandered up and down the crowded, twisty lanes between the booths, stopping to buy an orange or a handful of gilt gingerbread, or watch a dancing bear or a Cornish wrestler or a pedlar spreading out his pack of ribands and necklaces and embroidered sleeves, trying their luck at side-shows, greeting old friends and glaring at old enemies. Presently, when Nicky had won a pewter pot at the archery butts, and Argos had tried to fight a wall-eyed drover's dog whose face he did not like, they found themselves in the part of the Fair where books were sold (for Stourbridge Fair was a great place for books).

The others would have turned back to find something more interesting, but to Hugh there *was* nothing more interesting in the whole fairground. It was such a long time since he had seen even one book, that he was tempted to loiter and look at them longingly, while the Players sighed—at least, Nicky and Jasper sighed—and waited for him patiently, as he always waited for Argos when Argos could not make up his mind about the best place to bury a bone. There were a few huge, beautiful books bound in blue and purple and ver-milion; little clumsy books with blodgy woodcut pictures in them; thick dark books full of queer knowledge about stars and herbs, and many more. And Hugh wanted all of them, or failing that, just one—one little plain book to be his very own; but even the smallest and plainest cost more than he would possibly be able to afford, even if he saved hard all the while the Fair lasted. So at last he sighed and wandered off again with the others.

' It would be nice to be rich,' he said, ' rich enough to buy books, I mean.'

' What a queer cove you are, Dusty! ' said Nicky. ' D'you really mean to say that if you had the money, you'd spend it on books? '

' Yes, I *would*! ' said Hugh defensively.

' Every man to his own taste,' sighed Jasper, in an even more mournful voice than usual. ' If 'twas me, I'd buy a new pair o' shoes, with soles to 'em.'

Everybody laughed, even Hugh, and Jonathan said, ' I wonder which of you would have the more joy of your purchases.'

Not long after that they came to an open space with a man standing on a tub in the middle of it, and an interested and admiring crowd all round. He was a large, merry-looking man, with a round red nose and little twinkling blue eyes, and a very tall hat on the back of his head; and he was holding aloft a little box in one hand, and waving the other in wide, graceful flourishes while he talked at the top of a very trumpety voice.

' Here's Zackary Hawkins,' said Jonathan. ' There's not a quack doctor on the road to touch Zackary; he's a joy to listen to.'

So they joined the crowd and listened for a little while.

'I am not like those herbalists yonder, who will sell you bread-pills for your hard-earned money,' the Quack Doctor was saying. 'No. I have here the cure for all ills, which I discovered myself, at—ha! hum!—great personal risk, not to say inconvenience, and the secret of which is known only to me of all the teeming millions on this earth. Have you the backache? Have you no appetite? Do your arms and your legs ache, and do you feel all shiversome when you wake in the mornings? Do you suffer from colic, colds in the head or bunions? Have you spots before your eyes or a singing in your ears? Ha! Hum!—Then my Herbal Compound is the medicine for you! This box, my friends, is worth one hundred crowns! A hundred crowns is what my good friend the Archduke of Tuscany paid me for a box no larger; also the Califf Haroun El Mohamid, of the noble city of Baghdad, which is a very noble city indeed. But I am not one who loves money! No! The welfare of my fellow men means more to me than my own gain, and I have determined to sell my wonderful Elixir to you for only one crown a box! —No, for half a crown——'

Jonathan flung up one arm and waved, and the Quack Doctor saw him and waved back, but without stopping talking for an instant. 'No, for fourpence. The paltry sum of fourpence, my friends! Step up here, my friends, and . . .'

But the Players had slipped away, and were heading for a performing pony they could see in the distance.

'Does the stuff he is selling really cure all these things?' asked Hugh, looking back over his

D

shoulder at the Quack Doctor, who was still
shouting about his wonderful Elixir.

' Course not,' said Nicky, scornfully. ' It's just
powdered chalk.'

That seemed to Hugh very dishonest, and he
said in a disappointed voice, ' But he looked so
nice.'

' He is,' said Jonathan, looking down at him
with his queer faun's smile. ' Zackary's the
staunchest friend a man could have. He's a
thorough rogue, but *that* is quite a different matter.'

Hugh was still thinking this over, when there
began to be a great falling back and commotion
among the people all round him, and peering between the performing pony's master and an apple-
stall, he caught a glimpse of two or three stately
gentlemen carrying rods of office and attended by
several men who looked like the Watch, coming
towards them down the crowded alley.

' Steward's officers, by cock and pie! ' exclaimed
Nicky, and in the same instant Jonathan's hand
came down on Hugh's shoulder, swinging him
round to face the way he had come.

' Nip back to Master Hawkins,' said Jonathan's
voice in his ear. ' You'll get through this crowd
quicker than we could, and there's no time to
spare. Tell him the Steward's officers are coming.
Leave Argos with me.'

So Hugh gave Argos's leash to Jonathan, and
plunged away into the crowd. It was only a hundred yards at most, and all the way he could see a
red pennant fluttering from the roof of a booth
which he remembered had been close to the Quack
Doctor's stand, and quite a lot of the way he could

' *This box is worth one hundred crowns!* '

(See p. 73)

see the top of the Quack Doctor's tall hat. So he could not get lost. But the crowd seemed thicker than ever, and every moment he expected to be overtaken by the Steward's officers, and it seemed a very long time before he arrived. But he did arrive at last, breathless and buffeted, in the clearing where Zackary Hawkins was still talking at the top of his voice and handing out boxes of his Elixir from one of two large sacks beside him, and taking in the pence as fast as he could.

Diving and butting and sidling, and not stopping to apologize to people whose feet he trod on, Hugh reached the Quack Doctor, and gasped, 'The Steward's officers are coming. Jonathan sent me.'

Zackary Hawkins squinted down at him quite calmly, and broke off his trumpeting for one instant to say: 'Ha! Hum! Thanks, brother.' Then he began again, beaming at the crowd. ' My friends, you have had the last box! The very last box of my wonderful Elixir. But stay. I have here, for the ladies among you '—he plunged a hand into the other sack and brought out triumphantly a box that looked very like the ones he had been selling all along—' a little of the identical face-powder used by Helen of Troy to give lustre to her beauty when entertaining Julius Cæsar to dinner. Now, by a strange coincidence, this powder is almost exactly the same in appearance as my wonderful Elixir, so it is necessary to keep them carefully apart, since my Elixir applied outwardly, and this exquisite powder applied inwardly, would be useless; nay, worse than useless! Ladies, this is the identical face-powder used by Helen of Troy,

I do assure you! A friend of mine found it in the ruins of that city.'

Meanwhile, as soon as Hugh had disappeared in the crowd, Jonathan thoughtfully leaned against the apple-stall so that it upset, spilling a shower of russet apples all across the path of the Steward's officers as they came by. Nicky leapt to the rescue, and fell over the feet of the fattest officer, all but spilling him among the apples, and Jasper Nye, who was a good actor, even though he hadn't much sense, got in everybody's way, protesting almost tearfully ' Clumsy! clumsy! Oh, sirs, I trust you are not hurt.' While Argos wound his leash round the legs of another officer very cleverly indeed. By that time the performing pony was getting badly mixed up with the Watch, and the stall-holder was dancing with fury, the crowd were joyfully helping to gather up the fallen apples, and the Steward's officers were being most unreasonable and unhelpful; and altogether it was quite a long time before things got sorted out again and they could continue on their dignified way.

By that time they were very cross, and would have been only too pleased to find someone doing something they shouldn't. But when they came to an open space where a red-faced man was selling face-powder with a boy to help him, there wasn't anything they could do about it. There was no law against selling face-powder.

That evening there were cheerful gatherings round camp-fires, all over the fairground, for people had had the whole day to find old friends and now they were making merry together.

Hugh and the Players were joined by a good

many people that evening, and as they crowded round the fire, there was no merrier gathering of friends in the whole of Stourbridge Fair. Zackary Hawkins was there, with his hat still on the back of his head, and his little round red nose was shining like a cherry in the firelight; there were several players from another Company, and a tinker with a long red beard and a pedlar with a long blue nose, a juggler clad in tattered red-and-yellow fool's motley hung with bells, and quite a lot more. There was a Tom-o'-Bedlam, too. He did not know anybody, and nobody knew him; he had simply loomed up out of the dusk, a tall, wild figure, and sat down among them unbidden. Tom-o'-Bedlams were like that. Everybody accepted him quite happily, and he was given a share of their supper. It was a stew, and everybody except the Tom-o'-Bedlam had put something into it; the Players had put in fat bacon, the juggler had put in herbs and two eggs, the pedlar had put in a poached rabbit; and what with those, and all the other things, it really was a most beautiful stew with a most beautiful smell.

Nobody talked much over supper, but when the pot was empty and the company delightfully full, there began to be a great exchanging of the summer's news and a great making of plans for next year, all round the fire. Hugh and Argos were left to themselves, and Argos slept with his nose on his paws, and Hugh sat and hugged his knees and watched the others. Their faces were golden in the firelight, and behind them the darkness was purply-blue, like pansy petals; and the light of the leaping flames set tiny sparks dancing

in their eyes and made the rings in Benjamin's
ears and the bells on the juggler's hood and the
buckle on a strange player's hat all sparkle like the
jewels of the Lordly People.

The Tom-o'-Bedlam was singing to himself,
softly:

> 'With a host of furious fancies
> Whereof I am commander,
> With a flaming spear and a horse of air,
> To the Wilderness I wander.
> With a knight of ghosts and shadows
>   I summoned am to tourney
> Ten leagues beyond the wide world's end;
>   Methinks it is no journey.'

It was a song that all the Tom-o'-Bedlams sang
as they came and went along the roads, and Hugh
had heard it quite often; but somehow he had
never really listened to it before, and now that he
did, he found that it was magic: not at all the
sort that the Piper had made, for that had been a
very gentle magic, of sunlight and the open fields,
and this magic was dark and fierce and glorious,
and rather frightening. Suddenly, as he listened,
it seemed to Hugh that the night beyond the fire-
glow was crowded with enchantments and swirl-
ing with the Furious Fancies of the song; knights
in sheeny armour on horses whose leaf-edged trap-
pings trailed and swept through the darkness, and
marching armies of shadows, and griffons whose
wings spread and arched between the firelight and
the stars.

Presently he found that they were talking about
him; at least, Zackary Hawkins was. 'And so
we have a new-comer to the Company since last
year,' trumpeted Zackary Hawkins. 'A new

Brother, hey? A new member of the dusty-footed fraternity?'

'Aye,' said Master Pennifeather. 'And his name is Hugh. Hugh Copplestone. But maybe he's told you already.' For of course Master Pennifeather knew about the evening's adventure, and how Hugh and the Quack Doctor had already made each other's acquaintance.

Zackary shook his head so that his hat slipped slightly over one ear. 'Ha! Hum! No, he hasn't told me; didn't have much time for conversation this evening. Stand up, Hugh Copplestone; stand up and let's have a look at you.'

So Hugh stood up, grinning uncertainly, and everybody had a look at him. Nicky told him to turn round slowly, so that they could all see his front, and everybody laughed, because they were feeling full and lazy and ready to laugh at anything. And then, as Hugh turned round obediently like a joint on a spit, he found the Tom-o'-Bedlam peering up at him through the smoke of the fire.

Something about the deep-set, brilliant eyes of the Tom-o'-Bedlam made him feel odd all over; and the sort of half-joke suddenly stopped being any sort of joke at all. Argos seemed to feel the same; he did not lift his head from his paws, but the hair rose a little on his neck, and his eyes were like watchful tawny lamps in the firelight.

The Tom-o'-Bedlam rose in his place, and stood with his arms folded, towering over them like a King in all his rags. Not all very tall people look like kings, but this one did, at least he did to Hugh; the King of a lost country. 'Who stands friend for the New Brother?' asked the Tom-o'-Bedlam. 'Who speaks for him?'

And next instant Jonathan was afoot and standing at Hugh's side. 'I stand friend for the New Brother. I speak for him.'

'Who else?' cried the Tom-o'-Bedlam, peering about him through his wild hair. 'In all Brotherhoods, in all orders of Knighthood, it is decreed that there must be two to speak for the New Brother.'

For a long moment—and it seemed a very long moment to Hugh—nobody answered, because the rest of the Players were too busy grinning their heads off and nudging each other and waiting to see what would happen next. Then the Quack Doctor said 'Me!' and lumbered to his feet, with his hat sliding farther than ever over one ear, and came to stand at Hugh's other side. 'Lad's a good lad, and did me a good turn. Hum! Yes! I will speak for him,' said the Quack Doctor, patting Hugh on the shoulder.

Hugh glanced up at him gratefully, wishing he had never even *thought* about the Quack Doctor being dishonest, because Jonathan had been right, and he was a staunch friend, even if his Elixir of Life was only powdered chalk—stauncher than those grinning zanies round the fire, who thought it all so very funny.

'So,' said the Tom-o'-Bedlam, 'that is well.' He leaned down suddenly to stare into Hugh's face, his mad dark eyes blazing in the firelight. 'Have you kept your Vigil?' he demanded. 'Have you kept it alone, with none but the stars and the Ancient Ones for company?'

Hugh was so afraid that his mouth went quite
dry, but he stood his ground boldly, staring back
into the eyes of the Tom-o'-Bedlam; and then he
felt Jonathan poke him gently—like being poked by
the nearest person when they were playing and it
was his turn to speak next and he had missed his
cue. So he said, ' Yes, sir,' rather breathlessly.

' That also is well,' said the Tom-o'-Bedlam;
and swinging round on Jonathan, he demanded:
' Where is his knightly sword? Where are his
golden spurs? '

' His golden spurs were lost in a bog on the way
from Ireland,' said Jonathan instantly. ' And the
swordsmith has cut his hand and cannot finish the
blade until to-morrow.'

The Tom-o'-Bedlam seemed to be thinking this
over, and stood for a little while with his burning
gaze fixed on Jonathan's face; then he shook back
his wild hair and said, ' We must do without, then.
Give me the knife that you wear in your girdle,
friend.'

So Jonathan took the little bright dagger from his
belt, and gave it to him; and the Tom-o'-Bedlam
stooped and cut a small sod from the turf beside
the fire. Everybody had stopped grinning and
nudging each other, and they watched him in
silence as he turned back to Hugh.

' Hold out your hands, New Brother,' he demanded. ' Both of them—where are your man-
ners? *Both*, I say! '

And when Hugh hurriedly held out both hands,
he put the turf into them. ' Now swear fealty to
the Brotherhood. Swear by the white dust of the
road, and the red fire at the long day's end, and by

the thing that always lies over the brow of the next
hill.'

The bit of turf felt crumbly and damp in Hugh's
hands, and faintly warm from the fire; and still
rather breathlessly, he swore fealty.

' So,' said the Tom-o'-Bedlam. ' That is your
Seisin.   Seisin of the Road; Seisin of the Brotherhood.'

He drew himself up to his full splendid height,
and stood looking down at the gathering round the
fire.   Then he dropped the dagger on the trampled
turf, where it stuck point down, quivering and
gleaming in the light of the flames.

And before it had stopped quivering, he turned
away, flinging up his arms to the night sky with a
strange wild gesture that made his ragged sleeves
seem like wings; and as though he had suddenly
lost interest in the whole thing, wandered off into
the darkness.

As he went, they heard him singing again:

> ' With a knight of ghosts and shadows
>   I summoned am to tourney
> Ten leagues beyond the wide world's end;
>   Methinks it is no journey.'

Nobody moved or spoke until the strange song
had merged away into the night-time sounds of
the fairground.   Then Argos sighed and closed
his eyes, while the hair on the back of his neck
sank down again, and everybody looked at everybody else, and Hugh asked, ' What *is* seisin? '

' When you give or sell a piece of land to anybody,' said Jonathan, picking up his dagger,
' you give them a little bit of the turf from
it—give it into their hands, I mean—to seal the

bargain. That is seisin. It sort of *lets you in*, you
see.'

Hugh looked at the bit of turf in his hands. ' I
see,' he said. ' What do I do with it? '

' Put it back where it came from,' said Jonathan.
' It's only while it's being given that it matters.
You don't have to keep it afterwards.'

So Hugh put it back, fitting it carefully into the
little hole, and patting it down afterwards. Then
he asked: ' Is it always like that, when people come
to be one of the Dusty-Feet? '

' No,' said Jonathan, ' I'm afraid not.'

And Master Pennifeather gave a shout of laughter,
so that all the solemness and the splendour flew
away. ' Ye saints and sinners, no! That was just
Tom-o'-Bedlam up to his crazy tricks. Do you
think we should have left you to be spoken for by
Zackary here if it had been real? '

But it *had* been real in a queer kind of way, Hugh
thought, and Jonathan and the Quack Doctor had
known it.

' Anyhow, you're one of us with a vengeance,
now, my hero! Now that you've been given
Seisin of the Road,' said the juggler, looking up at
Hugh with little wise eyes as bright as the Morris-
bells on his hood.

VI

PAN AND THE STAR

ALL summer the sun had shone in a blue sky, but after Stourbridge Fair the weather broke, and it rained and rained all the autumn long. The roads turned from white dust to brown mud, and the tilt-cart sprang another leak in its tilt, which Jonathan patched with brown canvas, and got one or other of its scarlet wheels caught in a rut more often every day, and had to be got out by the whole Company, because Saffronilla could not manage it by herself. The roads were much emptier now, for nobody travelled in the winter unless they had to, but stayed warm and dry in their own homes; and so they passed no more gallants on horseback, nor ladies on mules or in coaches; and only the Dusty-Feet, who had no homes to stay in, were abroad in the wild weather.

They wandered south to St Albans, where they acted the Life and Martyrdom of St Alban, on the steps of the Eleanor Cross; and south again, between dripping hedges where the hips and haws shone like gay little lanterns through the driving rain.

'The Home Counties are best for the winter,' said Master Pennifeather. 'Sheltered country and plenty of towns and villages, and not too far between them.'

So they crossed the Thames again, and headed for Guildford Town. They acted their plays at

Sevenoaks and Tonbridge and Tenterden, and little friendly Kentish villages between; and at last they joined the road which is still called the Pilgrim Way, and followed it to Canterbury.

Hugh liked Canterbury, and he liked the Fountain Inn more than any of the inns at which they had stopped before. It was a rambling place, as many-roomed as a honey-comb, with lovely carved and painted garlands of vines and roses above little dark doorways. It had a painted sign swinging above the courtyard arch, to show that it was the Fountain; and a winter jessamine which the inn-keeper's wife had grown in her private garden had flung a lovely arch of yellow stars over the wall into the courtyard, like another fountain, all of gold.

Hugh was sorry when the time came to take the road again, but Jonathan said, 'We'll be coming back soon. We generally play in Canterbury at Christmas Time.'

And they did.

Three days before Christmas they were once more plodding along the Pilgrim's Way. The rain had stopped, but everything was very slushy and very green; and the people to whom they wished a Merry Christmas, in passing, all said, 'We're going to have a green Christmas, seemingly, not like the Christmasses when *I* was young.' Ben Bunsell picked a chilly primrose from the ditch, and stuck it in his bonnet beside the draggled peacock's feather. There was a small blustery wind that came and went when you least expected it, and little blurs of winter sunshine scudded about the meadows and orchards, and altogether it was rather a nice day, though certainly not very Christmassy.

But the road was soft and squelchy, and when they were just within sight of Canterbury, the tilt-cart got one of its scarlet wheels bogged again.

Everybody was so used to the tilt-cart getting bogged, that they went at once to their appointed stations, and put their shoulders to the back of the cart or hung on to Saffronilla's head to help her pull, making encouraging noises; and after a great deal of heaving and hauling, the wheel came out of the rut, and the gallant little cart was free once more.

' Phew ! ' they said, and mopped their foreheads; and then they noticed that Argos had disappeared.

' He was here a moment ago,' said Hugh, who had been one of the pushers-from-behind. ' He must have gone after a rabbit,' and he called, ' Argos, hi ! Argos ! ' but no Argos came.

' Hop on to the hedge and look around; he can't be far off,' said Master Pennifeather.

So Hugh scrambled on to the low bank, and looked round, whistling hopefully. ' I can't see him,' he called down to the others. ' You go on without me, and I'll come when I've found him.'

Nicky said, ' I don't mind staying to help you look for him. The others can make their entrance without us.'

And Master Pennifeather said, ' So be it. You know how to find the Fountain. Give that hound of yours a good belting with my humble compliments, when you do get him, Dusty. He's over-fond of this game.'

So Saffronilla and the tilt-cart and the rest of the Company went on down the Pilgrim's Way, while Hugh and Nicky scrambled through the hedge into the meadow beyond.

'There's a spinney over there; looks the sort of place he'd make for,' said Nicky.

So they set off for the spinney.

Hugh was not really worried at first, because Argos was rather bad about rabbits, and it was not the first time they had had to scour the country for him. But as it got later and later, and they found no sign of Argos, he got very worried indeed. They searched the spinney, and the country on both sides of the road; they worked their way along hedges and round hayricks and through meadows and orchards, calling and whistling as they went, and stopping to listen before pushing on again; but they heard no answering bark. Whenever they met a farm hand tramping home across the fields, they asked him, 'Have you seen a dog, a black-and-brown dog, very big?' But nobody had.

At last they stopped and looked at each other in the cold December twilight that was growing deeper every moment.

'Look here, Dusty,' said Nicky; 'it's no good going on now; we don't know the country and we'll never find him in the dark. The best thing we can do is to make for Canterbury; we'll have trouble getting through the gates if we leave it much later—and we'll come out again first thing in the morning.'

'You go,' said Hugh. 'I'll stay and have another look in the spinney. I must find him, Nicky. I must!'

'Well, you won't do it in the dark,' said Nicky, taking a firm hold on Hugh's shoulder. 'Besides, if I go back without you I shall be in trouble, and

I'm not going to do that for anybody. You're coming with me now.'

And after arguing miserably for a bit, Hugh went with him. It was quite dark by the time they found the road, and the wind was rising; and Hugh's inside felt as cold and cheerless as the night, as he trudged along beside Nicky through the thick mud. They got through the City gates without much trouble, and made their way along the narrow streets towards the Cathedral. The wind was blowing the clouds away and there were stars round the head of the Bell Harry Tower; but Hugh did not notice the stars, nor the Bell Harry pinnacles: he was too weary and worried and miserable, and the lighted windows that glowed so warmly under the steep black eaves of the houses only made him think all the more of the windy darkness back there in open country, where Argos was lost and alone.

When they turned into the courtyard of the Fountain, a stable-boy told them that the rest of the Company were in the stables; not in the fine new stables where they had slept last time, because those were full up with horses belonging to the fine folks, but in the old stables through the archway yonder. So Hugh and Nicky went through the archway, past their tilt-cart in a corner, to the old stables, which were low-ceiled and tumbledown, but very warm and welcoming after the wind and darkness outside. Saffronilla was in one corner, and Jonathan was walking round on his hands in another, practising his tumbling, as he did at some time every day, no matter how tired he might be, nor how many other things he had to do; and

the other three players were rehearsing by the
light of a stable lantern. But the moment the boys
appeared in the doorway, everybody broke off and
looked at them anxiously.

'You've not got him?' said Master Pennifeather.

Hugh shook his head without a word.

'And we've hunted the whole countryside,' said
Nicky, collapsing on to a costume basket and
thrusting out his weary legs in front of him.

Jonathan, who had come right way up again the
moment they appeared, took one look at Hugh,
and said very matter-of-fact, 'We'll all turn out
and look for him in the morning. If we divide
the country up between us, we're bound to find
him.'

Jasper Nye started to say something about not
being so sure, because they did not know the
country well, but the others glared him into silence,
and Master Pennifeather told the boys, 'Now you
go and get your supper and a warm before the fire,
and then come back here; we must rehearse the
pickling scene before we go to bed.'

So Hugh and Nicky went off across the dark
stable-yard to the inn, where a cosy-looking old
serving-maid in a gown of cherry-coloured linsey-
woolsey gave them each a bowl of stew and a place
in the chimney corner. 'Aye! ye poor babes.
Been out looking for the dog, have ye?' she said.
'I mind him from the last time he was here—a big
fine dog. He'll be all right, I reckon. Now sup
up your stew; 'twill put some heart into ye.' And
she bustled away to attend to other guests.

Hugh didn't want his stew; he was too miserable.

But Nicky made him eat it *and* wipe out the bowl
with his crust of bread; and when it was inside
him, somehow he did feel a bit happier, and began
to think that after all Argos was not likely really to
come to harm. For a little while they sat on their
heels before the fire, and when they were toasted
crimson they plunged out once more into the darkness and the bitter wind, and made their way back
to the old stables.

After that Hugh had no more time to be worried
or miserable for a while, because of rehearsing the
play they were going to act next day. It was about
St Nicholas, the Christmas Saint, and in the first
scene Hugh was a boy who was murdered by a
wicked innkeeper and cut up and put into a cask
to pickle, but St Nicholas, being told by an angel
what was happening, rushed up to the inn and
stirred up the pieces in the cask with a wooden
spoon so that they came together again and the
boy was as good as new. In the later scenes he
had to be a girl who would not be able to get
married because her father was too poor to give
her a dowry, until St Nicholas, passing the door,
heard her weeping and dropped a bag of gold
inside, so that she could get married, after all.
Jasper Nye was the old father, and Master Pennifeather was the villainous innkeeper and Jonathan
was the devil in scarlet tights who suggested that
he should pickle the boy; Ben Bunsell was St
Nicholas, and Nicky was the angel who told him
what the innkeeper was up to.

They all worked very hard to make the performance perfect, and it was quite late when
Master Pennifeather said, 'There, that's enough

for to-night, my lords and masters. Just remember to loosen *up* as you go into the cask, Dusty, and everything will be superb—completely superb! '

' Might as well go to bed,' yawned Benjamin. ' Early to bed and early to rise, *I* always say.'

' 'Tisn't early,' sighed Jasper, looking in a weary but admiring sort of way at his legs. ' S'late an' s'beastly cold.'

' That's the wind. It's blowing half a gale from the east, and the sky is ablaze with stars,' said Jonathan, who had opened the half-door of the stables and was looking out and up. ' It's not going to be such a green Christmas, after all.'

' Argos will be so cold,' said Hugh, who had had time to get worried again now that the rehearsing was over.

But Jonathan said, ' Not he! He's got a good thick coat, Brother Dusty-Feet.'

And Ben suggested cheerfully, ' You know, he might quite likely bring himself along here. He's a sensible beast, and he's been here before.'

Everybody had something cheering to say, as they piled up the bedding-straw higher yet, and kicked off their shoes. (They didn't take off anything else, it was too cold in the tumbledown stable, where little bitter winds whistled through the window and the thin places in the thatch.) And Jonathan came and squatted down beside Hugh in his corner, and spread a warm, rather greasy-smelling cloak over him.

' He'll be all right, you know,' said Jonathan.

' But it's so dark and cold and—and wintry—and perhaps he's fallen down a hole or something,' said Hugh, miserably.

Jonathan tucked the ragged cloak in under his chin, and said, ' Surely not. It's Christmas, and that is a very special time for animals.'

' You mean—because of the animals in the stable? '

' Ye-es, partly that,' said Jonathan, settling down into the straw.

Nicky blew out the lantern, and the darkness seemed like deep blue velvet, after the smoky yellow light. ' Jonathan Whiteleaf will now oblige with a story,' said his voice a moment later, rather muffled, as though he was talking with his head under the clothes.

There was a rustling and a settling down in the darkness, and then a hopeful silence. Jonathan was the story-teller of the Company, as well as the Doctor and the Playwright and the Tumbler between scenes, and the one who did most of the mending, and his stories were always worth listening to.

Even Hugh pricked up his ears, because he loved Jonathan's stories.

Then, ' I'll tell you a Christmas story, my masters,' said Jonathan's deep, quiet voice out of the darkness. ' I will tell you about the fourth guest who came behind the shepherds to the Bethlehem stable, that first Christmas.'

' Wasn't it a shepherd boy? ' put in Nicky's voice, muffled in the straw.

' Be quiet an' let him get on wi' th' story,' said Jasper Nye; and Nicky gave an apologetic grunt, and held his peace.

' People said it was a shepherd boy, after they had forgotten the truth,' said Jonathan. ' But I *have* heard that it was Pan, the master of all furred and feathered things, who followed the Star that night.' And he told them this story:

One autumn, when the field-mice and the tiggy-hedgehog and Brock the Badger were all making places for themselves to sleep in through the winter, Pan made a warm place for himself deep under the roots of an ancient tree. He lined it with rushes and fern, and curled himself up there to sleep through the dark, cold months until spring came again: just as though he was a harvest mouse, instead of the lord of all fur and fin and feather.

He fell asleep, and dreamed the things that the animal-kind do dream in their long winter sleep; until one night he awoke with a start. There was a tingling in his finger-tips like the tingling in the twigs of a withy when the sap rises, and something seemed to be calling him out into the world beyond his hole. At first he thought it was the spring, and he remembered the sun's warmth and young lambs crying and hawthorn smelling of cream and honey, and the long, hot days of summer to follow after. But the earth was still cold to his touch, and there was no whisper of seeds shooting and sap rising all around him; the mouth of his hole was narrowed with banked-up snow, and the stars that looked in at him through the gap that was left were bright with frost. It was still mid-winter, and Pan turned round again and tried to sleep.

But still something called to him, called and called from the world above, and Pan turned round once more, and looked up through the mouth of his hole; and suddenly all the brightness of the stars was gathered up into one great Star that shone straight into his eyes with a piercing golden light that made him blink. Now he knew what was calling to him; it was something to do with that Star, and he knew that he must answer the call.

So he gathered his hairy goat legs under him, and took his pipes, which had lain in the curve of his arm while he slept, and scrambled up through the opening of his hole, pushing his way through the snow that had drifted round it. All the world lay quiet, sleeping under the stars; the hills looked strange in their covering of snow, and the wind cut like a knife; but still the something was calling, as joyously as spring, and still the great Star burned and pulsed, hanging low out of the sky just over the scattered lights in the valley below, which he knew were the lights of Bethlehem. 'Whatever it is,' said Pan to himself, 'it must be in Bethlehem.' And he set out, leaping along over the snow, his great round hooves leaving a track behind him as though a huge goat had passed that way, and the golden light of the Star shining on the splendid sweep of his curved horns.

But he had not gone far when he heard a pitiful bleating and turned aside to see what it might mean; and in a hollow of the hillside he found a flock of sheep all huddled close together, outside their stone-walled fold, their eyes like green lamps in the light of the Star, and the mist of their breath hanging like smoke above them.

'What is the matter, my children?' asked Pan.

And the old scarred bell-wether pawed the snowy ground with a small sharp hoof, and said, 'Master, we are afraid. First there came a great light in the sky, and then a strange thing like a man with the wings of a golden eagle, and it spoke to our shepherds, and in a little while our shepherds went away, hurrying down the path to the town, without even folding us first. And now we smell wolf, and we are more afraid than ever!'

'There is nothing to be afraid of, my children,' said Pan; and he folded the sheep himself, and went on down the hill.

A little farther on, dark shapes loomed up suddenly all about him, and he knew that they were wolves. Savage and milky-toothed, their eyes gleaming red as hot coals in the light of the Star, they gathered round him, and the great grey leader came and nuzzled his head against him as a dog might have done.

'Whither away, Grey Brother?' asked Pan, rubbing him behind the ears.

And the pack-leader said, 'Yee-ow! Master, we smell sheep!'

'Turn back from your hunting,' said Pan. 'It is Peace to-night, my brothers.'

And an old she-wolf answered him: 'Master, if you say that it is Peace between us and the sheep-folk, then it is Peace, and we turn back from our hunting for to-night, even though our cubs are hungry.'

Pan watched them slink away into the shadows, and then he went on again, until he came out on to the valley road that led to Bethlehem. The trees were dark on either side, and the straight, white roadway ran between, with the golden Star hanging at the end of it; and Pan went on, following the Star. On the outskirts of the town he met

Still the great Star burned

(See p. 95)

three shepherds hurrying back towards the hills;
and one was old and grey, and one was brown and
of middle years, and one was young and golden.

' I have folded your sheep, whom you left forlorn
on the hillside,' said Pan wrathfully. ' It is a worth-
less shepherd who leaves his flock in the night time ! '

' We followed the Star,' said the golden shepherd.

' And it led us to a stable,' said the brown
shepherd.

' Master,' said the grey shepherd gently, ' a
Child is born to-night—a little King; and He is
greater than Pan.'

And they went on towards the hills where they had
left their sheep, and Pan went on following the Star.

In the narrow streets of Bethlehem the snow was
churned to brown slush by the many feet that had
trodden it, and Pan's tracks were lost among the
others. The sky between the roof-tops was turning green, for it was near to dawn, and soon the
stars would fade; but the one great Star burned as
brightly as ever, hanging low at the end of the
street. And the town slept, and there was no one
to see Pan go by.

On he went, up one street and down another,
following the Star, until at last it hung above the
stables of a tumbledown inn.

' This is surely the place,' said Pan. ' This is
where the thing is that called me.' And suddenly
a great awe fell on him; but he pushed open the
door and went in.

Inside was yellow lantern-light and the sweet
breath of the cattle wreathing upward. Mary slept
on the straw, and Joseph drowsed in the shadows,
for they were very tired; but the animals of the

stable were wakeful and restless, gathered about their manger to look at something that lay in it. An old red ox and a little grey donkey, a brown mare with her foal tottering on long, unsteady legs beside her, a half-starved dog and a tabby cat, and a ruby-combed cockerel who had fluttered up to perch on the edge of the manger itself. Pan could not see what it was that lay in the manger, but all the lovely feeling of spring that had called him from his sleep seemed to flow from it as light flows from a lamp.

The stable-folk knew Pan, and they parted to let him through, and as he passed between them, he saw, lying on the golden straw before the manger, a shepherd's crook, a ragged cloak, and a loaf of bread—gifts that the shepherds had left behind them for the little King. Then he was standing between the ox and the foal, with a hand on the head of each, and looking down with them into the manger. There was a new Baby in the manger, sound asleep; and as Pan gazed at Him, he knew that the grey shepherd had spoken truth, and this was the little King, and He was greater than Pan.

Pan squatted down on his hairy haunches, and leaned forward to gaze and gaze. All his heart went out to the little King, so that it hurt him inside, as he had never been hurt before, and yet he had never been so happy. Suddenly the Baby awoke, and lay looking up into the brown face, with the surprised, kitten-blue eyes that most very young things have. Then He smiled a small pleased smile, and made a small pleased kicking and waving with His legs and arms, and poked Pan's cheek with a tiny, crumpled fist.

There was a sudden sharp pain in Pan's breast and a sudden whimpering deep inside him, and he longed to weep, but he did not know why, for he was happy—so happy, that it was like the kindling of a light in a dark place. He put out one long, brown forefinger, and touched the little King very, very gently on one cheek in return. Then he got up and turned to go; but before he went, he laid his reed pipe among the gifts that the shepherds had left. 'He has a loaf for food, and a cloak for warmth, and the tool of a trade,' said Pan. 'And I will leave Him the gift of music, that is of the Spirit.' And he passed out from the stable into the chill of the dawn.

The dog went with him as far as the door, and licked his hand with a warm, loving tongue, to comfort him, and then padded back to the manger. And Pan went out alone.

Mary found the Pan-pipes among the gifts that the shepherds had left, when she awoke, and at first people guessed who had left it there; but as time went on, people forgot Pan, or rather they forgot that he was not just a legend, and they said, 'It must have been a shepherd boy, who left the gift of music for the little King.'

For a while nobody said anything at all, and then Nicky asked, 'Was that what you meant just now, about Christmas being a special time for animals?'

'Maybe,' said Jonathan.

And Hugh asked, 'What happened to Pan?'

'Who knows?' said Jonathan. 'Perhaps the animals do, but they wouldn't tell us if they could.'

VII

ARGOS

NEXT morning the Players turned out in a body before it was even light, to look for Argos, leaving word with the stable-hands to hold him if he should appear while they were away. They searched the country round for hours, calling and whistling, asking everybody they met, ' Have you seen a dog? A black-and-brown dog—very big?' But nobody had; and at last the time came when they must give up the search for a while, and go back to the Fountain to get ready for the afternoon's performance, because they had promised the good folk of Canterbury that they would enact the Life of St Nicholas that afternoon, and the show must go on.

They cut rehearsals that evening, and spent the time searching again over the country they had already searched in the morning, and next day they returned to the search yet again, but they had no better fortune than before.

It was Christmas Eve, and everybody seemed blithe and happy, hurrying here and there about their preparations for to-morrow's merry-makings. The wind had blown the last of the clouds away, and the weather had turned clear and frosty, and all the narrow streets of Canterbury were full of people carrying home great bundles of holly and ivy, bays and mistletoe and rosemary, for the decking of their houses. But the little band of

Players, grimly searching ditch and meadow and spinney which they had searched so many times before, did not feel Christmassy in the least, for they had all grown very fond of Argos.

Hugh would not go with anyone, not even with Jonathan; he went alone, searching in the same places over and over again, with his face very white and his eyes very black and his curly mouth straight and hard: calling and calling. But he didn't find Argos.

At last they had to give up and go trapesing back to the Fountain in a weary, dispirited little bunch. They were going to present the Shepherds' Play that evening, and they must get the costumes ready and see to the decking of the stage, and the lighting. Usually they acted their plays in the afternoons, as all Strolling Companies did, for it was not easy to light an open-air stage after dark. But on Christmas Eve they put on their play after star-time, and lit the stage as best they could with borrowed stable lanterns, because it was more festive to do it that way. So they collected up all the lanterns the inn would lend them, and there was a great cleaning of horn panes and sticking in of new candles, and a great decking of the stage with branches of evergreens, and a tremendous hurrying to and fro and up and down. It should all have been most gloriously exciting, but none of them had much heart for it, and poor Hugh was so desperately miserable that it screwed up his inside into aching knots and made him feel sick.

Argos was to have been a shepherd's dog in the play. They had spent hours teaching him his part, and he had learned it beautifully. And now they would have to do without him; and Hugh felt as though his heart would break.

At last everything was ready, and the bells of the Cathedral were ringing high overhead, calling people to the Christmas Eve service. Then the Players washed their faces at the horse-trough, and brushed themselves down and stuck sprigs of rosemary into their caps or the breasts of their jerkins, because they were going to church.

'You know,' said Master Pennifeather, scrubbing his face dry, 'it might be that the Egyptians have —er—acquired our Argos. He's a handsome brute.'

Jonathan was taking great care with his sprig of rosemary. 'To-morrow I'll go down to the Fighting Cocks Tavern,' he said. 'There's generally an Egyptian fiddler among the folks there; if they've taken him we'll get him back all right.'

'It's a trap I'm afraid of,' said Jasper Nye, gazing mournfully at his worn-out scarlet stockings.

'Be quiet, you idiot,' whispered Jonathan; and Nicky deliberately strolled across and thumped him on the head, just to show that he agreed with Jonathan.

'Yow!' yelped Jasper, rubbing the place. 'No need t'do that. I'm sorry. I jus' didn't think.'

'You can't; you never do. You're just a pair of lovely legs and nothing to think *with*. It's not your fault,' Nicky told him kindly.

But Master Pennifeather said, 'Peace, my lords! It's time we were away to church.'

And Hugh, who had been listening with his face half washed all this while, said wretchedly, 'I'd rather stay behind. Argos might come back and find us all gone.'

'The stable-men will hold on to him if he does,'
Master Pennifeather told him very firmly. 'No
member of my Company stays away from church on
Christmas Eve, Dusty, nor does he take with him as
much dirt on his—er—expressive countenance as
you seem to have on yours. So you'd best finish
washing it.'

So Hugh sighed, and finished washing his face;
and then they all set out.

Once in the street, they joined the gay crowds all
answering the call of the bells, and went with them,
up Mercery Lane and past the Buttermarket to the
lovely Christchurch Gate of the Cathedral. The
smooth grass of the Close was still grey with hoar-
frost in the shadows, but sparkling gold where the
winter sunshine fell, and the tall grey Cathedral
towers soared up and up into the blue sky; and
the music of the bells was so glorious and so loud
that the bell-tower and the naked elm trees in the
Close and carved kings and saints above the west
door all seemed to dance to it.

It did not seem as though anything unhappy
could happen at such a lovely time, when it was
Christmas Eve and all the bells of Canterbury
were pealing and rocking for joy in their high
towers, and the good people of the city were
hurrying to church in their gayest clothes and
their Christmas humours. And surely, Hugh
thought as he scurried along, Argos would be all
right—somehow—because of Christmas time.

The crowd was passing in through the great
west door, like a procession in a fairy tale, all in
their gayest doublets and farthingales of blue and
rose and saffron, and carrying little tight nosegays

of herbs; merchants and craftsmen and gentlemen, all with their wives and sons and daughters; prentice lads with sprigs of bay in their bonnets, and gay girls holding up their pretty kirtles to keep them clear of the mud; here and there a great lady with jewels on her fingers, and small, fat children being towed along faster than they wanted to go, and old creeping folk from the almshouses. On they went, and the Players with them, out of the winter sunshine into the dimness of the Cathedral, where the columns soared up and up, spreading into foamy curves and traceries high overhead, and the candles made a golden blur a long way off, and the stained windows glowed daffodil and azure and vermilion through the shadows.

The Players slipped into a humble place near the door, and knelt down. There were no pews or chairs in churches in those days, only a few benches for the most important people, and for the humble folk just hard stone floor.

People turned their heads to look at the six kneeling there in a row, for they knew them for the Players from the Fountain; and some people looked surprised to see them there, and some people drew aside from them as though they were afraid they might be catching, and some people looked as though they were thinking 'Rogues and vagabonds!' and wondering why the official dog-whipper did not come and get rid of them. But there were others who smiled at them nicely, and they were the only ones worth bothering about, after all. And one lady, in a mantle worked all over with little flowers like a summer meadow, turned out of her way and stooped down to them,

E

saying, 'You are the Players who have lost a dog, aren't you? I do hope you find him.' Then she went on towards the golden candle-glow at the east end.

It was a glorious smell of rabbits that made Argos slip through the hedge while everybody was busy getting the tilt-cart unbogged. He knew that he ought to ignore it and stay where he was, but it was such a beautiful smell. It whispered and pleaded in his twitching nose, and *would* not be ignored, though he did try. So he gave up trying, and slipped away like a black-and-amber shadow, through the hedge and across the meadow beyond.

The smells lay thick and low along the wet grass, crossing and re-crossing each other; all kinds of most exciting smells, and Argos dashed joyously along, following his nose. He did once hear Hugh calling him, but he was thinking so hard with his nose that he did not really notice what went into his ears. All the evening he hunted, following first one smell and then another, until the rising wind thinned them out and blew them away, and he remembered suddenly that he was being wicked.

The best thing, he thought, would be to find Hugh and the others as quickly as possible, and be very penitent. So he set off towards the road where he had left them.

Then it happened! One moment he was loping along very comfortably through the thick under-growth of a little wood, and the next, something shifted in the dead fern, there was a clash and a jangle, and two rows of rusty iron teeth were fixed in his fore-paw, bringing him down with a crash.

Argos

He let out a shrill yelp of pain, but it was all so sudden that just for a moment he was more surprised than frightened. Then he found that he was held fast. He dragged at the cruel trap until the hot agony ran right up to his shoulder, but he could not get free. He began to gnaw and worry at the iron jaws, until he had broken a tooth and his mouth was bleeding almost as much as his wounded paw; but the thing remained as firm as ever. He never thought of barking for help; dogs in traps very seldom do; he just lay and bit and bit at the rusty iron, while the pain in his paw grew steadily worse.

All night he lay there, shivering in the bitter wind, and sometimes whimpering a little for Hugh to come and take him out of the dreadful thing that would not let go his paw. But the long night wore away, and nobody came; it was not very likely that anybody would, for that trap had been set away back in the autumn by a man who had afterwards forgotten about it.

Morning came, grey and bitter and windy; and once Argos thought he heard Hugh calling, a long way off, up-wind, and he sprang up, not caring for the pain of his trapped paw, and barked and barked, quivering with joyful hope. But the wind blew his barking away, and the calling voice did not come any more; and Argos lay down and despaired, and then tore frantically at the trap, and then despaired again.

Night came once more, and the wind dropped to a frosty quiet, and the stars looked down through the twigs and the frost-rhymed brambles; the still cold crept into Argos so that the only bit of him

that was not chilled through and through was his
wounded paw, and that seemed to be on fire.
The stars grew pale, and it was another morning—
the morning of Christmas Eve. But Argos did not
know that; he did not know anything very clearly
any more. There was a queer cold drowsiness in
him, and he had given up biting at his trapped
paw. He was not even thinking about Hugh
now; he just lay still, his beautiful eyes filmed with
pain and hopelessness.

And then he heard the piping!

Not a tune, just single notes and little pauses, and
sudden falls like running water; very faint at first,
but drawing nearer through the trees. The cold
drowsiness left Argos, and he pricked up his ears.
He remembered that piping. It meant warm sun
and running on soft turf, and things to eat, and
Hugh's hands rubbing behind his ears, and the
smell of the south wind. Nearer it came, lilting
through the woodland ways, and Argos waited,
quivering as he lay, for now help was surely coming.
Then the piping stopped, and there was only the
silence of the woods left; no one coming, after all.
He could not believe it; he wagged his tail in
little, fluttering, apologetic wags. 'This is me!
Me in a trap! You *can't* be going to pass me by!'
And then, as the empty moments dragged on, he
suddenly flung up his head and gave one long,
despairing howl.

The piping did not come again, but light footsteps rustled through the dead fern, the bushes
parted, and a slight figure in green and grey and
russet rags stepped out from the shadows. Argos
looked up with frantic pleading whines into the

brown face with strange green eyes—green as spring itself—that bent over him.

'These men and their traps!' said the Piper, in a voice that was angry and sorry at the same time; and then, to Argos, 'Bide still, little brother,' and Argos did as the Piper told him, and stopped whining, for he knew that there was nothing now to be afraid of.

The Piper's hands were busy with the trap, doing strange and complicated things to it; and a moment later there was a jangling snap, and the iron jaws opened—and Argos was free!

He crouched shivering against the Piper's knees, rubbing his bleeding muzzle into the kind hands, while the Piper talked to him softly, calling him by name, for he remembered him, too, and gave him crusts of bread out of the rags at his breast, and examined his wounded paw.

'I shall not bind it up,' said the Piper. 'Lick it yourself, brother; it will heal better so.' Argos ate the crusts and looked up hopefully for more, but there weren't any. 'Nay, brother, I am no rich traveller to carry a banquet with me!' said the Piper, and he held Argos's damaged head between his hands and looked deep into his eyes. 'What am I to do with you? Where are your friends, small brother—the brown boy and the rest? Why have they left you in a trap?'

Argos wagged his tail and whimpered, explaining how wicked he had been, going off rabbiting so that his friends had not known where to look for him, but that he knew where to find them, and now, thank you very much, he must go and join them. He licked the Piper's hands for thank

you and good-bye, begging him to understand
that he could not stay just now; and the Piper
understood, and sighed. ' Go then, brother, go to
the brown boy.' And Argos went.

He went straight back across country, limping
along on three legs, to the place where the tilt-cart
had been stuck in a rut when he first smelled rabbits. Of course it was not there now, and after
he had run round in questing circles two or three
times, and sat down to think about it, he realized
that his friends had gone on. He remembered
which way they had been travelling, and when he
came to think of it, he seemed to remember the
road too. He had been this way before, and there
had been a juicy ham-bone at the end of it, and a
kind petticoat person who had given it to him.
So he set off down the road towards Canterbury, as
fast as he could go on three paws, which was not
very fast, because as well as the pain in his wounded
paw he felt queer and swimmy, and his legs did
not seem to quite belong to him. On and on he
went, feeling very queer indeed, but with his heart
high within him, because he was going to find
Hugh, until he saw houses ahead of him and came
to the dark tunnel of the City gates. Here and
there people turned to look at him as he passed—
a huge black-and-tawny dog with his coat matted
and his muzzle all cut and torn, limping by on
three legs. A red-faced man said, ' Get away, you
mangy brute!' and aimed a kick at him, because
he was the sort of person who likes to hurt anything
that is hurt already; and a nice little bunchy pink
girl said, ' Oh, your *poor* face!' and tried to fling
her arms round his neck. But Argos avoided the

man's kick and the little girl's hug, and went limping on his way, until he came to the archway of
the inn where he had stopped before. He was so
weak that he could hardly crawl along, but when
he saw the archway his tail went up and his head
went up, and he pattered in through it quite
jauntily, because he had got to the right place,
and any moment now there would be friends all
round him, and Hugh to love him and make his
paw well again; and he would never hunt rabbits
any more. He pattered across the courtyard,
looking round for his friends, but they were not
there, and though there was something there that
looked like the stage, it was all hung round with
evergreens, so that it smelled quite different from
the stage he knew, and he could not be sure of it.
He ran whining to the half-door of the stable where
they had all slept last time and sniffed along the
crack, but the smell inside was the smell of a strange
horse, not his own dear Saffronilla. And the black
certainty dawned upon Argos that they were not
there! He had come all that way to look for them,
and been so sure that they would be there, waiting
to take him back and love him; but they had gone
on and left him behind, and he was alone, quite
alone, in the black, howling world!

If he had only gone through the archway into
the inner yard, he would have found the tilt-cart
in its corner, and Saffronilla's smell under the
stable door; but he did not, and his poor heart
almost broke. He never heard the stable-men
calling to him, and when one of them tried to grab
him, he dodged past and bolted out with a howl
into the street again.

The street seemed a dreadful place, and he did not know where to go or what to do. He ran in and out among the crowds, sniffing and whining and looking for Hugh, lost and forlorn and very afraid. Then he came to another archway, and saw that a great many people were passing in through it, more and more people, until it seemed that all Canterbury must be going that way. Argos stood watching until the crowd thinned out and then, just as the very last of the people went by, he had an idea!

People trooping in through an archway like that always meant that Hugh and the others were acting a play somewhere near! Therefore he had only to go with the crowd and he would find Hugh! So he joined the tail of the procession, and went with it, in through the archway and across the open place beyond, to the door of a huge grey building that was not like any inn he had seen before.

Far off towards the golden candles, the organ began to play; but still people were trooping in, and the great Cathedral got more and more full, and still the people came. Then, when almost everybody who was coming *had* come, and the service was just that very moment starting, there was a rustling and a whispering among the folk nearest the door; and people turned round, and people pointed. The Players looked round too, and it was Argos!

Argos standing on the threshold of the great west door, with drooping ears and tail, and one paw held up, looking about him in a humble, frightened sort of way.

He saw Hugh at the same moment as Hugh saw him; and he gave a little joyous whimper, and Hugh gave a little husky cry; and next instant they were together in the open nave, Hugh with his arms round Argos's neck, and Argos rubbing his head against his master's breast.

'Oh, Argos, your *paw*!' whispered Hugh, but Argos didn't care about his paw because he had found Hugh again, and nothing else mattered in all the world.

Now, dogs were not really allowed in church in those days any more than they are now, and there were official dog-whippers to keep them out. But somehow everybody seemed to remember that it was Christmas, and they looked kindly at the great dog who had come, all lost and forlorn, to the Cathedral door on Christmas Eve; and even the dog-whippers pretended not to see him. So Hugh took him back to the rest of the Company, and after Jonathan had had a quick look at his paw, they sat down side by side; and Argos heaved a long, fluttering, exhausted sigh, and went to sleep, propped up against his master. Presently the others stood up to sing, and Argos roused a little, and kissed Hugh's chin with a warm, loving tongue; but neither of them got up, they just went on sitting bunched against each other and feeling so happy that it made them feel good as well.

They sat like that right through the Christmas Eve service, until it was over, and everyone was trooping out into the Close again; and the Players went with them, with Argos limping in their midst. It was drawing on to sunset, and all the world was flushing pink in the lovely sunset light, and the air

smelled of frost and woodsmoke and Christmas
Magic. The people streamed away across the
frosty grass of the Close, gay and laughing as they
made for their own homes and their own merry-
makings, and the little company of Players turned
aside under the bare trees to look properly at Argos's
paw.

'He's been in a trap,' said Jonathan, examining
the place, while Argos snuffled and whimpered and
licked his hand.

Everybody crowded round to look, in a sym-
pathetic way, and Ben Bunsell said, 'Then why on
earth didn't we find him? We've been over every
inch of the land hereabouts, I'll swear.'

'Easy enough to miss him,' said Master Pennifeather. 'We're not natives of these parts, to know
every pocket of the woodlands.'

'I wonder how he got away,' said Nicky.

And Jasper said, 'Wonder how a'knew where
t'look f'rus?'

Jonathan got up from seeing to Argos's paw, and
said, 'Somebody let him out—and he followed the
people coming to church.'

'Jonathan, oughtn't we to tie his paw up?' suggested Hugh.

But Jonathan shook his head. 'No. We'll bathe
it when we get back, but 'twill be better left open
for him to lick at himself. What he mostly needs is
something to eat.'

'Then let us repair to that hostelry from whence
we started out,' said Master Pennifeather in his
most high-flown manner, 'there to regale our
returned prodigal on the fat of rams.'

So they said, 'Come along, old man,' encouragingly to Argos, and set off for the Fountain, feeling as though all Canterbury belonged to them. The streets seemed gayer and more crowded than ever, and the smell of frost and woodsmoke and Christmas Magic grew stronger as the sunlight faded; the windows of the houses were beginning to glow yellow as marigolds, and here and there the sound of music lilted out from behind them.

When they got back to the inn there was a great deal of exclaiming and rejoicing, and the stable-men explained how it was that they had not been able to grab Argos when he arrived not five minutes after the Players had left for the Cathedral. The kind, fat maidservant came bustling out in her cherry-coloured linsey-woolsey petticoat, with a huge bowl of the loveliest bits and pieces for Argos; and when he was as full as ever he could be without bursting his skin, Jonathan brought warm water and bathed his paw. Argos didn't want his paw bathed, he simply wanted to go to sleep; so he cried a lot, although Jonathan was not really hurting him, for Jonathan was one of those people who can do painful things without hurting nearly as much as most people do. He cried to show everybody how sore his paw was, so that they should know how very brave he was being in not crying even more, and because it was nice to cry with Hugh to cuddle his head and say comforting things to him.

The moment Jonathan had done with his paw, he simply rolled over and went to sleep, and the Players left him where he was, and hurried across to the little dark harness-room behind the stage, to change for the performance. It was quite dusk by

that time, and their dressing-room looked warm
and welcoming in the light of one candle stuck in a
bottle. Hugh was playing the Angel Gabriel, and
after he had dived head-foremost into his saffron-
coloured tunic, Jonathan helped him on with his
wings. Whoever wore those wings had to have
help with them because they fastened just between
the shoulders where one could not reach the buckle
upwards *or* downwards. They were lovely wings,
made of real feathers, rather battered if you looked
at them closely, but from a little distance they were
superb—long and curved and powerful, blending
from white at the little, short, fluffy shoulder-
feathers, to deepest flaming orange—the colour you
see when you look into the heart of a crown-
imperial—at the long tip-most pinions. He had
just got properly fastened into them, and Jasper
and Benjamin and Master Pennifeather had just
got into the flowing burnouses of the three shepherds and were making up their faces; Jonathan
was putting on the brown robes of Joseph, and
Nicky was making himself look like an old woman
(for the beginning of the play was about a shepherd's wife who put a sheep into a cradle and pretended that it was a baby), and the noise of the
crowd gathering in the inn-yard was getting very
loud and cheerful, when there came a pattering of
paws and a whimpering just outside, and the door
was pushed open a little, and Argos's nose came
through the crack.

'Look! there's Argos!' said Hugh. 'He wants
to take his part.'

'The noble animal shall have his desire,' said
Master Pennifeather.

And Jonathan said, ' Good man, Argos! '

So Argos did take his part in the Shepherds'
Play, after all, and was the most tremendous
success!

It was quite dark before the time came for the
play to start; and the lanterns hanging along the
galleries to light people to their places glowed and
sparkled on the jostling crowd, and caught the
arching sprays of the inn-wife's winter jessamine
so that it shone like a fountain of golden stars.
There was even more laughing and shouting and
pushing than usual, because of it being Christmas
Eve. Master Pennifeather gave Hugh the long
golden trumpet that was always blown to announce
the start of the performance—because the Angel
Gabriel was obviously the most suitable person to
blow the trumpet for a Christmas play—and Hugh
climbed up the ladder on to the stage, with a great
feeling of importance and responsibility in his chest,
for he had never been trusted with the trumpet at
an actual performance before, although of course
he had been taught how to blow it. The people
stopped their shouting and pushing when they saw
the Angel Gabriel, and he raised the long golden
trumpet, flashing in the lantern-light, and blew the
most glorious and tremendous fanfare—the kind of
fanfare that nobody could blow unless they were
very happy indeed—with only one accidental
squeak from beginning to end. The lanterns in
the galleries were covered with cloaks, so that the
courtyard grew dark, except for the stage with its
green branches, which glowed in the light of four
stable lanterns, like an island of warm gold in a
dark sea.

Hugh turned and climbed down from the stage; and the Shepherds' Play began.

It was the best performance that had ever been in Canterbury. Everybody said so: the Players *and* the people who had watched them. But the people who crowded the courtyard of the Fountain that night remembered two things, afterwards, better than all besides. They remembered the Angel Gabriel standing alone on the empty lantern-lit stage, rather small, but so joyous that he looked as though he might spread his flame-tipped wings and soar straight up into the starry sky at any moment. And they remembered that when the shepherds came to see the little King, in the second part of the play, they brought their sheep-dog with them; a beautiful, proud, black-and-amber dog, who had a hurt paw and limped across the stage on three legs and poked his muzzle into the manger, wagging his tail as though what he found there pleased him most tremendously. Only, when the shepherds went away again, he would not go with them, but curled himself up against the Angel Gabriel's legs and went to sleep. And there he stayed right through the coming of the Three Kings, and all the rest of the play, not even waking up when the Devil in scarlet tights came to fetch the wicked King Herod at the very end.

VIII

THE MIST RISES

TOWARDS the winter's end the Company strolled down through the Kentish orchards and into the marsh country along the coast: Saffronilla clip-clopping along the marshland roads with the jaunty little tilt-cart lurching at her hairy heels and spilling things out behind; the Players trudging alongside, and Argos, whose paw had mended beautifully, generally trotting close under Saffronilla's nose so that they could talk to each other comfortably, which was nice for both of them.

There were not so many villages along the coast as there had been among the cherry orchards, but the people in the few villages there were, were friendly and seemed to like their plays, and they stayed in those parts until they got down to their last shilling. Then they decided to make for Rye.

One quiet grey noon the Players sat on the short coarse turf just beyond Burmarsh, in company with a shepherd and his sheep. They had turned off the road to pass the time of day with him and ask him the best way to Rye, where they meant to enact the Martyrdom of St Sebastian next day at the Mermaid Tavern. The shepherd looked as though he had stepped straight out of the Bible— shepherds very often do—with a long grey beard, and a hawk nose, and the skin round his wise old eyes puckered into a thousand fine wrinkles from screwing them up to watch his sheep in all weathers. He had been counting the flock when the Players came up, and they had waited, keeping a wary eye on Argos and the shepherd's dog, who were walking round and round each other, while he finished.

He used strange old words for his counting; words that sounded rather like a magic charm. 'Onetherum, twotherum, cockerum, quitherum, shitherum, shatherum, wineberry, wagtail, den,' counted the shepherd, and turned down a finger of his right hand before he began again: 'Onetherum, twotherum . . .' By the time he had come to the last sheep and used up all his fingers, Argos and the sheep-dog had decided to be friends.

Then Master Pennifeather had asked him the best way to Rye, and he had told them, and somehow they had got into conversation, and the Players had brought out their bread-and-cheese and the shepherd had brought out his; and now they were all sitting on the turf, eating in a companionable sort of way, while Saffronilla, who was used to being left to herself, cropped contentedly at the grass beside the narrow marsh road.

It was a little knoll they were sitting on, the kind of knoll you find sometimes in marsh-country, that has a tump of stunted thorn trees on it, so twisted by the wind that they looked like enchanted old men who stretch long, rheumaticky fingers inland all the year round, and wear white beards of blossom in the spring. All round them the marsh reached out and away, in soft blurred greens and greys, with the silver of many creeks and estuaries threading through it; so much silver that it looked

F

as though the whole marsh was sodden and might slip beneath the water at any moment. Away to the left was the great wall that kept out the sea, and the tiny bleak village of Dymchurch nestling under it as sheep huddle under a hedge for warmth when the wind blows over. There were no sounds but the lonely soughing of the wind, and the crying, calling wild-fowl, and now and then the shrill bleating of little new lambs among the flock, or the clink-clonk of the bell round the old wether's neck.

The shepherd was talking about the marsh in the tone of voice that people keep for the things they love most, and eating his bread-and-cheese and watching his sheep the while. 'Aye, the marsh looks ordinary enough now,' he was saying (though nobody had said it did), 'but when the mists roll up, 'tis another matter. Very quiet, they come, and very quick. Sometimes they comes smoking and wreathing up from the ground at your feet, seemingly, and sometimes they flows in from the saltings, like the ghost of the sea that used to cover all these parts. Many's the time I've stood on the high ground beyond Appledore in the clear night, and seen the mist flow up across the marsh, silver in the moonlight, with liddle waves in it, and liddle eddies, like as if the sea'd come back to claim Romney Marsh for its own again. The marsh isn't like other places in this world, not when the mist rises.'

'You're a poet, friend,' said Jonathan.

The shepherd shook his head, and took a huge bite out of his bread-and-cheese. 'Not me,' he said, when he had swallowed it. 'I couldn't make up a rhyme, not if you was to give me a golden rose-noble for it.'

And Nicky asked with his mouth full, ' I say, was all this really under the sea once? '

' Aye, but that was before my time; hundreds and hundreds of years before any time. The Romans came and pushed back the water from the marsh, so I've heard tell. They built the great wall, and they dyked it a bit, and they called it the Gift of the Sea. Ah, but the sea didn't give it willingly, and that's why it comes back, the ghost of a sea flowing up to the Weald where its old coastline used to be. And 'twould come back good and proper if we Marshmen once let it breach the wall—come flowing in, it would, spreading across our farms; and you'd hear the bells of the little marsh churches ringing under the water, not ringing to service no more, but just as the tide swung them, and none but the herring shoals to answer the call. That's the first lesson we ever learn, we of the marsh: " Serve God, Honour the Queen, but first maintain the wall." Only 'twas " King " when *I* learned it, for 'twas Harry the Seven in them days.'

They talked on for a bit, until all the bread-and-cheese was gone, and it was time for the Players to be going too. ' Well, we'll be on our way now,' they said, stretching and getting their legs under them.

But the old shepherd had begun to sniff the air like a dog scenting rabbits. ' I'd not go on to Rye to-day, not if I was you,' he said. ' There's a mist coming up. Better stop in Dymchurch.'

' We've already played in Dymchurch,' said

Master Pennifeather. 'We've played in every village hereabouts, and we're down to our last shilling. Therefore we must depart for an—er—more richly gilded neighbourhood, without delay; and we'll just have to take our chance of your mist, friend.'

' 'Tisn't much gold you'll find at the bottom of a dyke! ' said the shepherd, shaking his head. ' Don't say I didn't warn you! '

' We won't,' they promised.

And Ben Bunsell said, ' Beggars can't be choosers, *I* always say. And I suppose if we stick to the track we can't go far wrong, even in a mist.'

' I'd not be too sure of that,' said the shepherd. ' The marsh isn't like other places, not when the mist rises.'

Something in his voice made them feel a little prickly down their backs, but they certainly couldn't be choosers, with only enough money for one more meal before they put on their play in Rye; and if there really was going to be a mist, the sooner they were on their way the better. So they said good-bye to the shepherd, and set off.

At first the marsh lay clear all round them : long tongues of water reflecting back the sky, and the spires of the little marsh churches poking up from among the huddled roofs of villages here and there, and the marsh sheep grazing beside the sandy track, all very peaceful and friendly. Then quite suddenly there began to be a cold smell in the air, and a faint whiteness wreathing along the ground. The mist was coming up! It rose higher, flowing in from the saltings, with little waves in it, and little eddies, like a silent white sea; and before the Players had gone another quarter of a mile it was all about them, cold-smelling as the sea itself, blotting out the marsh in drifting swathes, so that they could see no more than a few yards of sandy track, and the coarse grass of the verge.

'Well, it's come all right,' said Master Penni-feather. 'Phew! what a witch's brew!'

'Good thing we've got a clear track,' said Ben-jamin. '"Fork left at the ruined barn," he said. And we can scarcely miss that, however thick the mist is.'

So they pushed on, quite comfortably, into the drifting whiteness.

'You know,' said Jonathan after a while, 'I think we've mislaid this barn.'

'I bin thinkin' that this past mile or more,' sighed Jasper Nye. 'Man said three miles, and we must've walked twice that.'

'You can't judge distance in a fog,' Master Penni-feather told him. 'Besides, people can never tell you the real distance to anywhere in their own countryside; haven't you learned that yet?'

So they trudged on again, until presently Master Pennifeather called back over his shoulder: 'Quite right, Johnnie, we *have* mislaid this barn. We shall have to cast back a bit, lads.'

It was rather difficult getting Saffronilla and the tilt-cart turned round on the narrow track, but they managed it at last, and set off back the way they had come. At least, they thought at first that it was the way they had come, but after a bit they began to have their doubts, especially when they came to a water-splash all across the track, which had not been there before. As they seemed to be on the wrong road, and were certainly travelling north when they wanted to go south, they turned off down the first track they came to that looked as though it might lead them in the right direction; but presently it began to run gently uphill, and Master Pennifeather, who was leading the way, said: 'It looks to me as if we're getting too far towards the Weald.'

Jonathan and Hugh were just behind him, and Jonathan suggested, 'That might be a good thing. We'd get clear of this mist, on the higher ground, and we could skirt the marsh and come down on Rye from the landward side.'

Everybody thought that was a good idea, so they pushed on again, rather wearily by now. Sometimes the mist lifted a little, and showed them a patch of sodden grass or a twisted gorse-bush, but always it came down again as thick as ever. Then the track dipped again, and got very pebbly, and suddenly through the drifting mist-wreaths they caught the glint of water, and Jonathan and Master Pennifeather were just in time to stop Saffronilla, who was half asleep as usual, from plunging straight into it. They were on the edge of a tidal pool!

'This is ridiculous!' said Master Pennifeather, when they had got Saffronilla safely back on to the track which forked just there, with the pool in the fork of it. 'We were heading for the Weald.'

'An' we've got to the sea,' Jasper pointed out helpfully.

They all stood and looked at each other, rather blankly, through the mist that seemed thicker than ever. That was when they noticed the silence; a

They were on the edge of a tidal pool!

(See p. 126)

queer, cold silence; no sea-birds crying, no bleating of young lambs, no wind soughing through the short grass of the saltings, nothing but the water making tiny stealthy sucking sounds among the reeds. It was not a nice silence, and the longer they stood still, the worse it got.

'Look here,' said Jonathan at last. 'A track can't go on for ever without getting to a village, and at least this left-hand branch seems to turn inland; let's follow it and see what happens.'

''S'my belief these marsh roads *don't* get anywhere, not when the mist rises,' said Jasper. 'I don't like it.'

Nobody else liked it either, but it was no good just standing there on the edge of that lonely pool, so they took the left-hand track and trudged on again. It was bitterly cold, and soon the February twilight began to turn the mist from white to grey, and it was hard not to wander from the path. Once they met a half-wild sheep, who stared at them as though they were the first humans ever to pass that way, before she tossed her head and flung away into the mist; and once a curlew rose crying from the bents almost at their feet; but otherwise they might have been the only creatures alive on Romney Marsh. It was a very desolate feeling. Presently the drifting mist-wreaths seemed to take on queer shapes, and the Players found that they kept on wanting to glance over their shoulders, just to make sure that there was nothing behind them. Argos kept on pricking his ears too, as though he heard things; but *they* could not hear anything but their own footsteps; those, and the silence. . . .

Hugh kept very close to Jonathan, very close

indeed. ' I expect we'll find a village quite soon, don't you, Jonathan? ' he said carelessly.

And Jonathan said, ' Sure to, Dusty.'

For a long time (at least it seemed a long time) they struggled on; but they did not find a village. And then, when they were getting really desperate, the mist suddenly thinned out into a kind of tunnel, and there at the end of it they saw the low black huddle of a house and outbuildings, rising straight out of the marsh with no garden or hedge of any sort between it and the loneliness. Just for an instant they saw it, by the last light of day and the glimmer of the rising moon, and then the mist rolled back and blotted it out. But they thought they had caught the flicker of a firelit window.

The Players halted and looked at each other as well as they could; they all knew queer stories about people who got lost in lonely places at night, and then found a house—a strange, dark house, maybe, with firelight in its windows, and perhaps the sounds of dancing lilting out through them— which was not there at all, in the daytime. ' The marsh isn't like other places, not when the mist rises.' But they were past caring about old stories.

' Let's risk it,' said Jonathan. ' I'll go and knock, if you'll wait here for me.'

And Master Pennifeather said: ' As leader of this band, I shall—er—take the lead in this affair. Never shall it be said that Tobias Pennifeather should have been called Tobias *White*feather! Besides, if two of us go, we can fish each other out of the dykes on the way.'

So it was arranged, and they set off; only it was four of them, because Hugh was not going to be

parted from Jonathan, and Argos was not going to
be parted from Hugh. They plunged away into
the mist in the direction in which they had seen the
dark house, keeping a sharp look-out for ditches
and pools; but the coarse grass was firm under
their feet, and they had only gone a few yards
when they began to catch the glimmer of the firelit window through the drifting mist-wreaths, and
after that it was easy.

When they reached the black wall of the house,
they scouted along it until they found the door,
deep-set like the door of a fortress, with the firelit
window glowing warm in the darkness right above
it. And when they found the door, Master Pennifeather beat upon it with his clenched fist. The
tattoo sounded very loud, in the silence of the misty
marsh; and an instant later there broke out such
a baying and barking inside the house that the
hearts of the three Players jumped uncomfortably,
and the hair rose along the back of Argos's neck.

' Ban dogs,' said Jonathan wearily.

And Hugh grabbed Argos's collar with both
hands.

But beyond the strong door, a tremendous voice
was raised above the din. ' Quiet, Roland!
Quiet, Oliver! Plague and pestilence, stop that
noise!' The baying stopped, and at the same
moment, somebody who had been whistling ' Jenny
Pluck Pears ' broke off to proclaim in a very harsh
voice, ' St George for Merry England and the Dons
to the Devil!' and then went on whistling.

' This would seem to be a strange household,' said
Master Pennifeather, uneasily.

But at that moment the door was jerked open,

firelight and torchlight flowed out like a welcome, and a little old man, who looked rather like an aged billy-goat, appeared on the threshold, peering out at the Players under his hand. 'Well, and what might you be wanting?' asked the old man, not so much surly as just plain dismal.

Master Pennifeather began to explain. But Hugh hardly noticed the goaty old man at all; he was staring past him, up the great glowing hall beyond, to another man who stood with his back to a roaring fire at the far end; a huge man, tall and broad and immensely fat, with curling red hair and beard, and a face like a round crimson sun. Two huge mastiffs lay at the man's feet, nose on paws and eyes watchful; a little white cat clung to his left shoulder, her tail waving gently behind his ear; and perched on his right shoulder was a strange big bird, rather like a hawk—but such a hawk! Its breast was the colour of a crown-imperial, its wings and mantle were deeply blue, and it was whistling 'Jenny Pluck Pears'. Hugh began to feel as if he must be dreaming.

'We are Players who have lost the Rye road in the mist,' said Master Pennifeather, doffing his bonnet with very nearly his usual flourish. 'And chancing upon this house, we make so bold as to beg the shelter of your barn for the night, knowing that the dwellers in the marsh are—er—famous for their hospitality.'

The goaty old man began to say something, but they never knew what, because the fat man let out a roar that shook the rafters. 'Players, is it? Splendid! Barn, is it? Not to be thought of! Come in with you! Players, by the Lord Harry,

and just in time for supper! Never was there
such good luck! Come in and shut the plaguy
door!'

They explained that there were three more of
them outside on the road, and a horse and cart as
well, and before they knew what was happening a
shock-headed boy, who seemed to be called Silly-
Billie, had been summoned from the kitchen by
another roar from the fat man, and sent off to
collect the rest of the Company and see about
stabling Saffronilla; and Jonathan and Master
Pennifeather had been gathered to the fire by a
wave of the fat man's enormous arm. But Hugh
hung back a little, with his hands still twisted in
Argos's collar, and an eye on the two mastiffs who
had got up and were advancing on him slowly, just
in case there was going to be a fight.

'Hi! Boy!' shouted the fat man. 'Is that dog
a fighter?'

Hugh shook his head. 'No, sir, not often.'

'Neither are Roland and Oliver, so you can let
him go. Let him *go*, my good lad, before you
strangle his eyes clean out of his head; and come to
the fire a'mercy's sake!'

So Hugh let Argos go, and came thankfully to the
fire, and squatted down, holding out his wet, frozen
hands to the crackling flames. The three dogs
walked round each other on very stiff legs for a
few moments; then Roland sneezed, and Oliver
sneezed, and they both went and sat under the
table, while Argos simply folded up where he was,
and went to sleep. So that was all right. But
the little white cat was not at all sure that she liked
Argos, and she stood up on her master's shoulder,

arching her back and watching him with wide,
amber eyes; and the strange blue-and-gold bird
seemed quite sure that he did not like Argos at all,
and flapped his wings and crooked his neck to peer
at him balefully out of one eye. 'Hurrah! Hurrah! Bring me that man's liver!' said the blue-
and-gold bird.

The Players jumped and looked round; and the
fat man flung back his head with a roar of laughter
that made the little white cat almost lose her
balance. 'That's Arthur!' he said. 'That's Lord
Grey de Wilton! Folks mostly jump when they
hear him for the first time. Did myself, for that
matter, never having met one of his sort before.'

'If you please, sir,' said Hugh when he had got
over his surprise, 'do they all talk like that—his
sort?'

'Couldn't say, I'm sure; never having met
another one. Very rare in England, these painted
foreign birds,' said the fat man, holding up a finger
at which the bird nibbled. 'My boy Ned brought
him home for me from foreign parts. Had some
outlandish foreign name, by the Lord Harry! And
couldn't speak a word of English. But we soon
changed that, and he talks the Queen's English
like a Christian now!'

'Hurrah! Hurrah!' said the foreign bird, still
peering at Argos.

Everybody laughed, and Jonathan said: 'And
certainly he bears a famous English name'—for
Lord Grey de Wilton was a renowned soldier, and
the Queen's deputy in Ireland.

'My oldest friend,' nodded the fat man. 'And
I named the bird after him because they're

uncommonly alike; both got hooked noses, both got
vile tempers—Ah, but I remember Arthur Grey as
a lad, when he was as mild and obligin' as—as I
am myself! We served together at St Quintin;
that was before he got his wound. Made a worse
hole in his temper than it did in his leg, that
wound!' He swung round on the goaty old man,
who had been scuffling in and out all this while
setting the long trestle table for supper, and raised
his voice in a bellow that made a log fall out of the
fire. 'Plague and pestilence, Timothy, where's
the cold beef? Am I to wait all night before my
orders are attended to? Am I, or am I not master
in my own house? By the Lord Harry, I said cold
beef, and I mean cold beef!'

Timothy brought the cold beef, a huge round of
it, which he set on the table with a sigh and a
clatter; and almost at the same moment the rest
of the Players arrived, shaking the mist-drops from
their bonnets and blinking in the sudden light; and
the fat man gathered them all in with shouts of
welcome.

Soon after that, without knowing quite how it
happened, they were all sitting down to supper off
the cold beef and crusty bread, herb cheese and
apple pasties, and brown ale foaming in leather
jacks. They had found by that time that the fat
man's name was Mr Thomas Trumpington, and
his little cat's name was Nimminy-Pimminy; and
they had told him theirs in exchange, and it was
all very friendly and comfortable.

Mr Trumpington sat in his great chair at the
head of the table, with Nimminy-Pimminy on one
shoulder and Lord Grey de Wilton on the other,

and pressed more and more food on his guests, and ate enormous slices of beef, and talked and talked with his mouth full—mostly about his boy Ned who was serving under the real Lord Grey in Ireland just then, but also about navigation and the price of wool and the habits of barnacle geese. And the Players sat and ate their supper, and did not talk much, partly because they were so very tired and hungry, and partly because they were a little dazed at finding themselves honoured guests so unexpectedly, and partly because Mr Trumpington never stopped, and they could not have got a word in edgeways if they had wanted to.

Hugh, sitting beside Jonathan, with Argos's head on his knee under the table, still felt as though it was all a dream. But if it was a dream, he hoped he would not wake up yet a while, because it was such a nice one. As the darkness deepened beyond the one high window, the long hall glowed more and more warmly in the red light of the fire and the smoky yellow light of the torches that never reached the great roof-beams and the thatch high overhead. And somehow it seemed all the more sheltering and friendly because of knowing that the wreathing mist and the silence and the loneliness of the marsh were still outside. It was like being safe inside a golden shell; and the apple pasties had cloves and cinnamon in them and were the nicest that Hugh had ever tasted.

Then quite suddenly Mr Trumpington leaned forward, beaming at them so that his round face looked more than ever like a crimson sun. 'When will you be ready to begin?'

'Begin?' they said.

'The play! The play, by the Lord Harry!' said Mr Trumpington.

They had not really expected to put on a play that night, but they couldn't disappoint Mr Trumpington after eating his beef and apple pasties. So Master Pennifeather said they could be ready in an hour. (There was a big brass lantern clock in the corner.) And Mr Trumpington said, 'An hour? An hour it is by the Lord Harry! And you'll be wanting an audience; oh, yes, I know; and an audience you shall have!' He began counting on his fingers. 'There's myself, Roland and Oliver, Arthur and Nimminy-Pimminy; that makes five. There's Timothy and Araminta; that makes seven. And the four farm lads; that makes eleven if you count Silly-Billie—he's not quite right in the head, but no matter, he'll be perfectly happy as long as he can bring his ferret.' He let out a sudden bellow which brought a surprised spider tumbling out of the thatch on to the table, and Timothy scuttling from the kitchen with a 'What is it *now*?' expression on his face.

'Timothy, we're going to have a play here in the hall. We're going to have it at eight o'clock, and everybody is to come and watch it. *Everybody*, mind!'

'Me too?' said Timothy dolefully.

'Plague and pestilence! Did I, or did I not, say everybody?' demanded Mr Trumpington. 'Send one of the lads down to the village to fetch me Parson Treadgold as well.'

Timothy shook his head. 'I'll *send*, but I doubts if Parson Treadgold'll *come*; not in this mist, not to watch Players. 'Tisn't as if 'twas a game of chess.'

Mr Trumpington banged both fists on the table until the pots and platters hopped. 'Bring me Parson Treadgold!' he roared. 'By the Lord Harry! Am I, or am I not, master in my own corner of the marsh? Show me the man who dares to contradict, and I'll have that man's liver! Bring me that man's liver, I say, and bring me Parson Treadgold, or I'll have your liver too!'

Everybody sat up joyfully and waited for more; and Lord Grey de Wilton got very excited and began sidling up and down his master's shoulder with his wings half spread. 'St George for Merry England and the Dons to the Devil! Hurrah! Hurrah! Hurrah! Bring me that man's liver I've got the gout coming on again Ned!' squawked Lord Grey de Wilton.

So Timothy went off, sighing, to collect the household and see about fetching Parson Treadgold, and Mr Trumpington helped himself to another apple pastie and said: '*That's* all right, then. But I wish my boy Ned was here; it's little enough junketing he'll be getting, sitting in an Irish bog.'

The next hour was a very busy one. The Players unpacked the costumes by the light of a stable lantern—the St George costumes, because Mr Trumpington had chosen the True and Noble History when they asked him which play he would like—and brought them in in glistening armfuls to the closet that had been given them for a dressing-room. They shifted the great trestle table with Mr Trumpington's help, and cleared a space before the closet door to be their stage. Then they started to change; and while they were changing, with the closet door ajar so that they should know what was going on, Parson Treadgold arrived. A tall, thin old man, with a stoop and a long, gentle face, who looked rather pained when Mr Trumpington thumped him on the back, bellowing, ' No chess to-night! Something better than chess, to-night, by the Lord Harry! ' and pushed him violently into a great chair beside the hearth.

Hugh watching him with interest through the crack of the closet door, saw that his stoop was just the same sort as his own father had had; the scholar's stoop that comes from poring for a life-time over books. And suddenly he remembered Oxford again: all the towers and spires of Oxford framed in the splendour of the rainbow. Just for a moment he saw it quite clearly; and then he found that Nicky was thumping him violently on his behind, and telling him to get on with his changing, and stop mistaking himself for Peeping Tom. So he thumped back, and finished pulling on the green stockings he was wearing as the Populace.

Then the rest of the audience that Mr Trumping-ton had promised came trooping in, and pulled their forelocks and settled themselves on stools in the fire-glow, Timothy looking more doleful than ever, and Araminta, who was fat and cheery, wiping her red arms on her apron; and the four farm lads with their faces shining from being washed at the well. Silly-Billie's ferret was sticking its head out of the breast of his shirt and looking about with its bright ruby eyes. Mr Trumpington sat in their midst, with Roland and Oliver at his feet, and Nimminy-Pimminy and Lord Grey de Wilton on his shoulders. The torches had been put

out, and the hall was full of crowding shadows between the fire-glow at one end, where the audience
sat, and the taper-light at the other, where candles
of fine Italian wax had been set to light the make-
shift stage. And everybody drew a deep breath,
and waited.

Then Jonathan pushed open the closet door,
stepped out into the glimmering radiance of the
candles, and raised the long golden trumpet that
reflected back the candle-flames in dancing stars
of light. The notes of the fanfare sang and echoed
through the long hall, humming among the roof-
beams as the note of a struck bell hums in its belfry,
long after Jonathan had stepped back, and the King
of Egypt in his mantle of French rose-scarlet had
come forward to speak his opening lines.

From Jasper as St George, to Hugh as the Populace, the Players gave their very best that night, to
please Mr Trumpington, because he had treated
them as honoured guests instead of rogues and
vagabonds. And the play was a very special
success in consequence, even though Silly-Billie's
ferret escaped in the middle and they had to break
off for a little while to help catch it. When they
got to the great fight between St George and the
Dragon, there was a positive uproar! Mr Trumpington leaned forward in his chair, beating his
fists on his knees and cheering them both on to
victory, while Araminta shrieked joyfully and the
farm lads shouted and whistled; Roland and Oliver
barked and Lord Grey de Wilton pranced up and
down, squawking, 'The Dons to the Devil! Hurrah! I've got the gout coming on again Ned!'
Even Parson Treadgold said, 'Very nice. Very

nice, I'm sure,' as though he really meant it.
Only Timothy looked as dismal as ever; and
Nimminy-Pimminy carefully licked her paw and
washed behind one delicate ear, as though such
vulgar junketings were quite beneath her notice.

When it was all over, and the Company had
lined up to bow, Mr Trumpington began to roar
again. 'The hat! The hat! *I* know how these
things are done! This is my affair, my party!
Bring me the plaguy hat!'

So Jasper brought him Ben Bunsell's hat with its
broken peacock's feather gleaming like a jewel in
the firelight, and Mr Trumpington felt in all his
pockets, puffing a great deal, and then put something into it. It was only one coin, but it gleamed
yellow in the bottom of Ben's hat. A half-angel!
More than they could have got in pence if they
had been playing to a packed inn courtyard!

'Because the audience is small, by the Lord
Harry, that's no reason why you should go with
empty pockets,' said Mr Trumpington, waving
aside their thanks so violently that he hit Parson
Treadgold on the nose by mistake, and made the
poor man's eyes water. 'If my boy Ned had been
home, the audience would have been one larger,
anyway.'

Soon after that the gathering broke up. Mr
Trumpington offered Parson Treadgold a bed for
the night, but he said he preferred his own, and
went off to it, through the mist, with Silly-Billie
and his ferret for escort, to see he got there safely.
Then their host said good night, and went away
with Nimminy-Pimminy and Lord Grey de Wilton
still riding on his shoulders; and the Players

settled down for the night, wrapped in their old cloaks in the warm rushes before the fire, with Roland and Oliver to keep them company.

Next morning the mist was gone, and the marsh lay clear once more, green and grey and silver, with little glints and gleams of gold where the February sunshine caught the ripples of the creeks and tidal pools. And after saying good-bye to Mr Trumpington the Players set out again for Rye, with the half-angel clinking against the few silver pence in Master Pennifeather's pouch.

' Well, we *did* find gold in the marsh mist, in spite of the shepherd's warning, my lords, even if it wasn't in the bottom of a dyke,' said Master Pennifeather, jingling the pouch triumphantly.

' I do hope his boy Ned comes home soon,' said Hugh.

IX

THE FINE GENTLEMAN

AFTER a while the little Company turned west-
ward along the coast and the Downs, where
the turf was thyme-scented underfoot and
the fat clouds sailed like stately galleons overhead. Presently they came into Southampton.
They did not do at all well in Southampton because the citizens had not the sense to know good
acting when they saw it, and did not appreciate
Jonathan's tumbling either; so the Players started
out again after two days, instead of staying three,
as they had meant to do.

When they came to pack up the tilt-cart, Master
Pennifeather served out drum and sackbut, as usual,
for they always marched out of a town to music,
just as they marched in: a good exit being just as
important as a good entrance, as every Player
knows. Jasper Nye said he didn't see no point in
making a noise about their going, when they
hadn't anything to make a noise *about*. But Master
Pennifeather said, 'What? Sneak out like thieves
in the night, and allow this—this city of the Philis-
tines to think we care a snap of the fingers for its
scurvy treatment? No, my lords! Not while we
have wind to blow with!' And so they marched
out through the great Westgate, between Wind-
whistle Tower and Catchcold Tower, and away for
the New Forest, to the brave music of drum and
sackbut playing 'Mary Ambree', with their legs

straight and their heads up, though their belts were pulled uncomfortably tight because they had not been able to afford breakfast and would probably not be able to afford supper either. Saffronilla was the best off, really, because she could eat grass.

They did manage supper, after all, because they found a village on the forest verge, and acted the Martyrdom of St Cecilia on the grass plot before the ale-house, afterwards passing round Benjamin's feathered bonnet.

It was early spring by that time, and the forest was flushing deeper every day with the lovely bloomy purple that comes when the sap is rising. There were golden catkins dancing on the hazel sprays, and the goat-willows tufted with silver; the blackthorn was breaking into a froth of starry white all along the woodshore, and the buds were thickening on the great forest trees—oak and ash and thorn trees that looked as though they had been old when William Rufus hunted the red deer through the woodland ways.

The Company spent a long time in the forest, wandering from village to village, for there were many hamlets tucked away in clearings and on the edge of open commons, and the people in them were glad of the chance to see a play. So the Players always had an audience of some sort, though often enough it was a very little one. Besides, the forest was a nice place to be in, in the spring.

One morning a great gale arose; the wind roared and sobbed through the trees, and the branches lashed together, and all the forest seemed full of the noise of a wild sea, racing cloud-shadows and flying bursts of sunshine; and now and then huge branches came crashing down into the road, so that really it was not safe to be abroad. Saffronilla did not seem to mind at all, but just plodded on comfortably through the hurly-burly, with the tilt-cart lurching at her heels. She never minded anything, except people sneezing, which she minded very much indeed. But Argos was dreadfully frightened, and insisted on walking between Hugh and Jonathan, and being talked to all the time.

About mid-day they came to a hamlet. It had an ale-house with a bush over its door for a sign, and a church with a pepper-pot steeple, a few cottages pressed back among the trees, and a lot of tall thin pigs, and the stocks just outside the churchyard gate for putting evil-doers in. It had a rude, buttoned-up sort of look that was not welcoming.

' This,' said Master Pennifeather, ' does *not* look promising.'

' Best push on t'the nex' village,' agreed Jasper, gazing at the hamlet with a face that was nearly as rude and buttoned-up as its own.

But they couldn't push on, because round the next corner they found a great tree lying across the road, with its poor broken roots in the forest on one side and its budding branches in the forest on the other. There were deep ditches and dense undergrowth at either side, and they couldn't possibly get Saffronilla and the tilt-cart round or over. There was nothing for it but to turn back to the buttoned-up-looking village.

' Oh well, what can't be cured must be endured, *I* always say,' said Ben Bunsell consolingly, ' and the roads are most unsafe, anyway—trees falling about in that careless way.'

The ale-house was not nice, nor was the landlord. They were both dark and dirty, and they had most disagreeable expressions. The landlord said yes, they could take Saffronilla and the tilt-cart round to the stables at the side, and yes, they could have bread-and-cheese for dinner; but he sounded as though it hurt him to have to let anybody have anything they wanted.

So they took Saffronilla and the tilt-cart round to the stable-yard, and sat on the shafts of the cart and the edge of the horse-trough, to eat their bread-and-cheese.

'This is a beastly place,' said Nicky, glaring at the cheese, which was mouldy.

'Ne'er the less, we shall have to stay here, friend Bodkin,' said Master Pennifeather. 'And we shall have to present the Martyrdom of St Cecilia here, if we're going to sup this evening.'

Jasper Nye muttered something about wishing St Cecilia was boiled, and stared mournfully at a mangy cat that stared mournfully back at him. They had been playing St Cecilia rather a lot lately, because her costumes were uppermost, and therefore easiest unpacked in the cramped quarters of little forest hedge-taverns, and Jasper was very tired of her.

'Are we as poor as all that?' asked Benjamin.

And Master Pennifeather said, 'My lords, I have the supreme honour to inform you that we shall have fivepence halfpenny in the world, after the bread-and-cheese is paid for.'

Just then, above the howling wind, they heard a sudden clatter of horses' hooves, and a voice yelling for the landlord; a gay, laughing voice with a

strong Devonshire accent that made Hugh prick up
his ears and sit still with his hunch of bread-and-
cheese half-way to his mouth. The voice was de-
manding a meal and a fresh horse; and the landlord's voice, not nearly so surly as it had been when
he spoke to the Players, was protesting that there
wasn't a fresh horse to be had, and offering the
parlour and fried ham. Then the voice seemed to
have gone indoors, and they heard it through the
window, telling the landlord that his house wasn't
fit to keep crossbred ferrets in.

Everybody listened happily, and next moment a
short, cheerful-looking manservant came into the
stable-yard, leading two horses. One of the horses
was walking lame, which explained why the gay
Devonshire voice had wanted a fresh one.

The manservant was a friendly soul, and as
there was no stable-man, Jonathan helped him with
the horses, and doctored the damaged hock of the
lame one, who slobbered lovingly against his
shoulder while he did it. Horses always loved
Jonathan, and so did dogs.

'Anyone'ud think you was her master,' said the
manservant, and he told them how he and his
master were riding down to Plymouth and the
mare had gone lame, and now they would be held
up in this dog-hole of an ale-house until next day,
there being no fresh horse to be got before then.
But for his own part, said he, he wasn't sorry,
misliking the forest in such a gale, and having no
wish to have his head scat open by a falling branch,
whatever his master thought about it.

When all the bread-and-cheese was done, Master
Pennifeather got up and stretched, saying that he

would go and ask where the nearest Justice of the Peace was to be found, so that they could get a licence to play that afternoon.

Quite soon he was back, looking rather worried, and said that the local Justice was away visiting his married daughter at Ringwood. Everybody looked at everybody else, and thought ' No supper '.

' Well, what d'we do now? ' asked Jasper.

But it was the friendly manservant who told them. ' Put on your play, lads,' he said, ' and hope for the best.' And he darted off towards the house, in answer to a sudden yell from his master.

' He's right,' said Benjamin. ' Nothing venture, nothing gain, *I* always say.'

' Yes, we know you do,' they said; but they agreed, all the same, and they set to work in a great hurry to unpack the costumes and set the raised grass plot before the ale-house door in order for their stage, while Master Pennifeather went off to cry the play through the village. They changed their clothes in a little dark room which the landlord had grudgingly lent them, and by the time they were ready a little crowd had begun to gather. Jonathan went out first, with the long golden trumpet, and taking his stand on the grassy stage, sounded such a fanfare that even the hurly-burly wind seemed to grow quiet to listen. The manservant was there already, and at the sound of the trumpet another figure lounged out through the ale-house doorway and joined the throng of country folk. A very gorgeous young gentleman in a doublet and hose of kingfisher blue, and a velvet cloak lined with pearl-coloured satin. He had a long curling feather as deeply green as the heart of the emerald fastened into his bonnet by a golden clasp, and his eyes were the brightest and bluest that Hugh had ever seen. Hugh wondered if the Anthony Heritage whose servitor his father had been at Oxford, and who had hated learning and spent so much of his time in Bocardo, had been like that. Somehow he thought he must have been. But there was no time to think of that, or anything else, but the play just now.

The play began; but it had not got far when the village constable arrived. 'You stop that!' said the Constable, who had a pimply face and a glittering eye. 'You've got no licence from His Honour the Justice.'

Master Pennifeather bowed with a flourish. 'Finding that His Honour the Justice was from home,' he said, 'and feeling sure that he would not wish us to go supperless to bed while he disports himself at his married daughter's, we made bold to dispense with the licence. You may tell him so with our blessing, when you see him.'

The Constable let out an enraged bellow, and poked a large and nobbly stick at them. 'Don't 'ee dare speak to me like that! You take off them funny clothes, you vagabonds!'

'Vagabonds, is it?' cried Master Pennifeather with superb defiance, while the crowd shouted joyfully. 'Sir, have you no soul, no sensibilities, no *decency*, that you presume to use such language to the shining lights of the English stage?'

'No!' said the Constable. 'You stop 'opping about; you're going to sit in the stocks, you are.'

'It's no good talking,' muttered Jonathan. 'We'll have to fight.'

And Hugh began joyfully to kilt up St Cecilia's skirts, while Nicky, who was also playing a girl's part, did the same.

Fight they did, for at that moment the Constable, with the landlord and a party of foresters at his back, charged them, shouting to the rest of the villagers to join in.

It was a glorious fight! Shoulder to shoulder the little brotherhood held the grassy stage against the whole village, for by that time everybody had joined in, because, much as they had liked the play, they liked a fight even better. Hugh and Nicky, Ben and Jonathan fought with bare fists, Master Pennifeather with one property stool and Jasper Nye with the other, which they wielded like two-handed swords; Argos fought with bared milky teeth, and the young gallant and his man, who had somehow joined them, with hedge-cudgels they had thoughtfully taken away from two villagers on their way through.

'Stand by to repel borders!' sang the young gallant, bringing his hedge-staff down with a joyful crack on the head of a burly forester.

'St George for Merry England, and Perdition take all constables,' replied Ben Bunsell, hitting out at another.

Jonathan was fighting in grim and bright-eyed silence and doing a good deal of damage, and Hugh kept close to him. It did not matter being rather shorter than most of the enemy, Hugh found, because the grass plot being raised, he was on higher ground than they were; and he managed beautifully, and made the Constable's nose bleed.

They were the Spartans holding the Pass of

Thermopylae against all the hordes of Persia; they were the crew of an English ship beset by Barbary Corsairs; they were the Last Stand of the Scots at Flodden. But, like the Scots and the Spartans and the English crew, they were outnumbered ten to one; and more people were arriving every moment to swell the ranks of the attackers. They fought long and valiantly, but they were pulled down at last, bruised and bleeding. Argos was half stunned and had a coat thrown over his head before he could bite anybody else (he had bitten several people quite badly), and they were all hustled off, still struggling, in the direction of the stocks.

Of course they should not have been put in the stocks until they had been brought before the Justice; they should have been put in the lock-up. But the lock-up was part of the Constable's cottage, and if there were people in it who kicked and shouted (as the people in the lock-up generally did), it was very disturbing for the Constable, and he did not like being disturbed. Besides, it was much more fun for the village to have them in the stocks.

So the Players were forced down on to the long bench, and despite all their kicking, the foot-board was clamped down on their legs, and locked.

'Well, we've made our mark on this village, anyway,' remarked Master Pennifeather with satisfaction, looking round at the broken heads and battered faces of the enemy, who were tying the struggling Argos to the foot-board with a short piece of rope.

'Yes, but they've made their mark'n us, too, *an'* th' St Cecilia costumes!' sighed Jasper, who was always inclined to be easily down-daunted.

It was a glorious fight!

(See p. 149)

But Ben Bunsell dabbed gently at his nose, and pointed out, 'Well, you was wishing St Cecilia was boiled. You can't have it *both* ways. 'Sides, think what a lovely view of your legs you're going to have in these stocks!'

'There, me beauties, right and tight you are, and there you'll sit until His Honour comes home to-morrow,' said the Constable; and he went home to his supper, taking the key with him.

But the rest of the villagers did not go home to supper yet. They gathered round and stared. The Players stared back, with their noses in the air. The young gallant and his man had somehow disappeared, and they did not blame them. It had been very nice of them to take their side in the battle, and you couldn't expect anyone to sit in the stocks for fun, not for the sake of perfect strangers.

'Come on, lads,' shouted the villagers, and began to throw things—not at all nice things.

'Human nature is a sorry thing,' said Master Pennifeather, wiping the remains of a rotten egg out of his left eye. (Rotten egg stings.) 'These people enjoyed our play, accepting what we had to give them, and now that we are under—er—a temporary disadvantage, they enjoy themselves even more by throwing rotten eggs. Ingratitude, thy name is—by the way, what *is* the name of this village?'

'Haven't th' least idea,' said Jasper. 'Only I know I never want t'see it again.'

Jonathan said, 'Keep your head down, Brother Dusty. Yes, I know it doesn't look so well, but if you keep it down you're less likely to get hurt.'

Jonathan had sat in the stocks a great many times before, and knew about these things.

Hugh had not known that people's faces could look so stupid and cruel, and he minded their faces and their harsh jeering voices even more than he minded the things they threw. Hugh had not sat in the stocks before.

It was really rather beastly while it lasted, but after a time the light faded and it got hard to throw straight. One by one people began to slip away and go home to their suppers in the cottages whose windows were beginning to be full of firelight; and the Players were left alone in the gathering darkness.

After that it wasn't so bad. It was cold, of course, and the gale still surged through the trees, roaring and beating its wings above them, and humming through the bell louvres in the church-tower high overhead; but close under the church-yard wall they were sheltered, and the long grass around the stocks only shivered now and then. Darker it grew, and darker yet, and Hugh, sitting beside Jonathan in the stocks and the windy darkness, screwed round to watch the firelit windows glowing from the cottages away beyond the church. The windows were gold and orange and apricot-tawny, criss-crossed by the shapes of the lashing boughs, and somehow the warmth of them was comforting to the cold emptiness of his inside.

But presently the lights began to go out, one by one, until only a saffron warmth in the window of the ale-house was left; and then that went out too.

'The fine gentleman would seem to keep early hours,' said Master Pennifeather.

G

It was very dark after that last light had gone, and it seemed to Hugh to get suddenly colder.

'Lean against me, and try to go to sleep,' said Jonathan, and put an arm round him.

So Hugh snuggled up to him as well as he could, and tried to go to sleep, because he always did what Jonathan told him. But he could not manage to get the least bit sleepy; he was too cold and empty and his bruises ached too much; anyway, stocks were not comfortable for sleeping in.

After a time the moon rose, full and round and silver into a sky that showed deepest blue between the shreds of scudding silver cloud; and with the moon came the Fine Gentleman. They did not see him come, because he walked in the dark shadows at the side of the lane, and they did not hear him, because the hurly-burly wind drowned his footsteps, but suddenly he was there.

There was a large rent in the shoulder of his beautiful cloak, and by the flying moonlight they could see a dark smeary-looking bruise all along his cheek-bone, but somehow he did not look disreputable, as the Players did; he seemed to be one of those people who always look neat and tidy, like Hugh's periwinkle.

Argos did not bark at him, as he generally did at strangers who came near in the dark, partly because he was half strangled by the rope round his neck, but also because he remembered that this particular stranger had been with him and his master in the battle. Instead, he wagged his plumy tail and whined throatily. For a moment the Players and the Fine Gentleman gazed at each other in the moonlight, and then the young man

swept them a low bow, one hand on the hilt of his
long rapier.

'Good evening to you,' said he. 'I congratulate
you, one and all!—I came to offer my condolences,
and I find you sitting in a row, seemingly as comfortable as Aldermen at the Lord Mayor's banquet!'

'Though something emptier,' said Master Pennifeather.

'Ah, I was afraid of that,' said the Fine Gentleman, fishing inside his doublet. 'Alas, we have no
time for eating just now. Gentlemen, I have the
honour to bring you the key of the stocks,' and he
fitted something into the heavy lock, while the
Players simply sat and goggled at him.

Master Pennifeather was the first to get his
breath back. 'Ye saints and sinners! How did
you get that?' he gasped.

'Oh, I got it off the Constable,' said the young
man airily, raising the foot-board. Everybody
stretched their cramped legs and groaned in
ecstasy, while Hugh and Jonathan made haste to
untie Argos. 'It was quite simple,' he added,
putting the key back in his doublet. 'I told him
he couldn't go round locking up bunches of Walsingham's secret agents without getting himself
into trouble and probably into the Tower, but that
if he gave me the key, I'd arrange for your escape,
and hush the whole thing up. He was very glad
to give me the key after I'd described to him the
sort of dungeons they have in the Tower.'

Everybody gazed at the Fine Gentleman in
admiration.

'Walsingham's—secret—agents!' murmured Jasper Nye, wagging his head.

'And he *believed* you?' said Jonathan.

'Of course. You're just the sort of people who might be, you know' (which was quite true. All sorts of queer people up and down the country, and in foreign lands too, were spies in the pay of Mr Secretary-of-State Walsingham). 'And now, if you've got your legs back into marching order, we'd best collect the cart; Will Squance should have done loading up by now, and the sooner you're clear of this parish, the better.'

He was a very masterful young man, and they trooped after him like children after the Pied Piper, back to the ale-house. The tilt-cart, ready loaded, stood in the middle of the stable-yard, with Will Squance sitting on the shafts. He got up, grinning, when they appeared, and said, 'You've got 'em safe then, Maister Walter.'

'I've got them,' said the young man. 'Now to see them safely out of this hornets' nest.'

Jonathan said quickly, 'You'd best be getting indoors, master. You've done enough for us already, and 'twill do you no good to be found in our company; that story about our being Walsingham's men won't stand much looking into.'

But the young man only laughed. 'I shan't be found in your company. The whole village is abed and asleep by now, and there's no fear of our waking them, in this wind.'

They got Saffronilla out of the stable and into the shafts without any trouble, the howling gale drowning the clippity-clop of her hooves and the trundling wheels as they led her and the cart out into the lane.

'I'll come and see you on your way,' said the young man.

So they said good-bye to Will Squance, and set out together, back the way they had come that morning, for the road beyond the village was still blocked.

In a small silver clearing amid the lashing darkness of the forest, a long way from the unfriendly village, the little Company halted. A wind-ruffled stream ran through the clearing, and the Players bathed their cuts and bruises thankfully in the swift, cold water; but they did not wait to change out of the tattered St Cecilia costumes before beginning on the food which the Fine Gentleman had produced from the tilt-cart where Will Squance must have put it.

The Players had not expected any supper that night, but they had not known how hungry they were until they saw the bread-and-cheese and cold bacon. They shared it out in a great hurry, and settled down on the grass, while the Fine Gentleman sat on the edge of the cart and watched them, with his arms akimbo and his battered bonnet on the back of his head.

'Blessings on your head, my lord!' said Benjamin, with his mouth full.

Master Pennifeather reached for the cheese, and asked, without any of his usual high-flown air, 'Why have you put yourself out like this, for such as we, master?'

'Fellow feeling,' said the Fine Gentleman, blithely. 'I do not like constables, and I like good fighting men. Also I gathered from Will that it was empty pockets that made you put on your play this afternoon without a licence, and I am—er—somewhat empty of pocket myself. Fellow feeling, yiss!'

They looked at him. They saw the gold clasp in his bonnet and the silver lace on his cloak, and the long, slender, velvet-sheathed rapier at his hip, and they did not believe him in the least.

The Fine Gentleman seemed to know that they didn't believe him just as though they had said so, and he laughed in a joyous, crowing way.

'Nay, but it's the truth I'm telling you! It comes of having expensive tastes.' And then, suddenly becoming tremendously eager, he leaned forward on his perch, making quick wide gestures with his hands. 'But I shall be rich one day!' he said. 'I shall have as much gold as the Incas of Peru! And not only I—England shall have it too. When that day comes we shall build a more glorious England, and everybody will be happy!'

They thought perhaps he was mad, but if he was, it was an exciting sort of madness.

Master Pennifeather asked, 'And how are you going to get so much gold?'

And the Fine Gentleman said, 'Make it, of course. Three times already I have almost discovered the Elixir, and each time I have made a slight mistake and had an explosion instead; but I know exactly what I did wrong last time, and next time I shall make no mistake at all.'

Then of course they knew that he was not mad, but only one of those people who believed that if you found the right Elixir to do it with, you could turn ordinary metals into purest gold. Lots of people believed that, in those days.

'What shall you do with your gold when you have made it, master, besides building a new Heaven and a new Earth?' asked Jonathan. Jonathan did not believe that anyone ever would find how to turn ordinary metals into gold, or that it would be at all a good idea if they did.

All at once the Fine Gentleman's face went quiet in the moonlight, quiet and far-off looking; and he said, 'I shall fit out tall ships, and sail them into the West, to win for the Queen a greater Indies than those of the King of Spain.'

Something turned right over inside Hugh, and he swallowed a piece of bacon in such a hurry that he almost choked, and begged: 'Oh, *please* tell us about the Indies.'

So while they finished their supper, the Fine Gentleman told them, shouting above the wind. And the spell of his words lifted them up and carried them along with him, so that the wild wind and the ache of their bruises were forgotten, and the bread-and-cheese seemed a royal banquet, and the stars crowded down through the flying cloud-wrack and the lashing boughs, to listen. He told of wide green plains, and great falls of water taller than church steeples that filled all the river-gorges with spray through which the sun made rainbows; and rich land where English settlers could make another and richer England, if they got the chance. He told, too, about the cruelties of Spain: how King Philip was trying to claim all that wonderful country for himself, and selling the natives into slavery and robbing them of all their ancient treasure, but how Englishmen would one day drive the Dons out of the Indies and take them for the Queen's Grace, because it was black shame that Gloriana of England should not have a greater Indies than Philip of Spain. . . .

At last, when the bread-and-cheese was all finished, he broke off his spell-binding, and got up from the edge of the cart; and the glory faded and the wind swooped back. It was time for the Players to be on their way.

'Take the lane that leads off to your left, about a mile farther on,' said the Fine Gentleman. 'And turn left again at the cross-tracks, and by dawn you'll be in a village that will appreciate good acting. I know this part of the forest.'

So, standing with their bonnets in their hands, they thanked him, each and everyone, for having stood their friend, and for their supper; and Master Pennifeather asked: 'May we know your name, sir?'

The young man bowed, doffing his own bonnet. 'Willingly. I am Captain Raleigh—Walter Raleigh—lately returned from service in Ireland, and very much at your service,' he said. 'And now, good night to you, and good fortune, my friends.'

They watched him swinging away down the road village-ward, sometimes lost in the black tree-shadows, sometimes clear in silver moonshine, until he disappeared altogether.

Then they turned their faces towards the next village.

'What a queer fellow!' said Nicky, after they had trudged a little way in silence. 'Nice queer—but queer, all the same!'

And Master Pennifeather shook his head, and

said: 'Aye, and what will he do if he doesn't catch up with those dreams of his, my lords?'

'I think that in that case, maybe he will die for them instead,' said Jonathan, very softly, so softly that the wind blew his words quite away, and only Hugh, who was nearest to him, heard what he said.

The day came, years later, when the Players liked very much to tell people that Sir Walter Raleigh had once fought in their ranks, and afterwards rescued them from the stocks. And years and years later still, when Queen Elizabeth was dead and the new King had made a shameful friendship with Spain, and the glory was gone from England, and Sir Walter Raleigh did die for his dreams, on a scaffold in Old Palace Yard, Hugh remembered, as though it were only yesterday, that wild, moonlit night when the Fine Gentleman had drawn the hearts out of their breasts with his talk of Golden Indies. And he was very, very glad of that night, ever afterwards.

X

ST GEORGE AGAIN, AND A
GREEN DOUBLET

JUST beyond Shaftesbury, on a grey, drizzly
morning, the Players found a foreign sailor.
At least, it was Argos, galloping ahead, who
found him first, and he was sitting in the damp ditch
all among the primroses and starwort, looking as
glum as a moulting blackbird, and nursing an injured
foot.

Argos stood in front of him, staring very hard,
and blowing his cheeks in and out in a friendly
sort of way, and wagging his tail, and the foreign
sailor stared back at Argos, and went on nursing his
foot. Then Saffronilla and the tilt-cart came round
the corner of the lane with the Players trudging
alongside, and they all saw him.

'Yon fellow would seem to be in trouble,' said
Master Pennifeather, and he went on ahead while
the rest followed more slowly. (Saffronilla did not
like hurrying.) They saw Master Pennifeather
speak to the man, and the man show him his foot,
and as the tilt-cart drew alongside, Master Pennifeather called, 'Hi! Jonathan, here's a job for
you.'

So Saffronilla stopped, and immediately fell
asleep, and Jonathan crossed the road and knelt
down in the ditch to look at the foreign sailor's
hurt, while the others gathered round to watch.
They had known he was a sailor from the first

moment they saw him, because of the seaman's red bonnet on his curly black head and because all his clothes had a seafaring look about them, but they had not known that he was foreign until they came close enough to see his olive-brown face and his bright black eyes that made them think of the Italian puppet-masters they sometimes met on the road. He had a deep cut in the sole of his foot, and Jonathan said: 'That is an ugly gash. How did you come by it, friend?'

The sailor smiled uncertainly, and shrugged, and pointed to a sharp stone with a crimson stain on it, that lay in the wet grass nearby. 'I 'ave wore thin the soles of the shoes,' he said in slow, careful English. 'The stone, it come through.'

'Dusty,' said Jonathan, 'go and get me the pot of salve from the cart, and a clean rag.'

Hugh darted off at once, and began rummaging in the tilt-cart. It took him rather a long time to find the salve, and even longer to find a clean rag, especially as Argos had scrambled in beside him and was trying to help; and when he came back with them, the rest of the Company were sitting in the ditch too, and Jonathan was bathing the sailor's foot with water fetched in Nicky's hat (it was better than Ben's for carrying water in) from a pond nearby that had water buttercups and green pondweed growing on it.

'I've brought the salve, Jonathan,' said Hugh, 'and here's a bit of rag—it's the cleanest I could find.' And he sat down on his heels to hold the pot for him and watch what he did with it.

Jonathan finished bathing the foreign sailor's foot, and spread salve on it, and bandaged it up with the bit of rag. 'That feel better?' asked Jonathan.

'Thanka you, yes. You are—ver' gentle,' said the sailor politely; and he drew his legs under him and began to get up.

'You can't walk on that foot,' Jonathan told him.

'But I 'ave to reach to Bristol,' said the sailor in a bothered voice.

'Our ways be together as far as Glastonbury,' said Master Pennifeather. 'You'd best come with us and ride in the cart.'

So they took a few things out to make room for him, and the foreign sailor came with them, riding in state in the back of the tilt-cart, with his bundle beside him, and his feet swinging just clear of the road behind. He travelled with them in that way for several days, and they grew to like each other very well; and in return for the ride he helped them with the making and mending and contriving of costumes and properties, for he was clever with his fingers, as sailors generally are. He told them that his name was Paolo, and that he was from Genoa, and that he had come to England often and often, but never seen more than the seaport towns his ship called at, until this time he had determined to see something of the country. So he had got leave from the Shipmaster, and left his ship, the *Santa Lucia*, at Poole, meaning to rejoin her at Bristol. He told them, too, about his voyages and adventures, and about his little farm inland from Genoa, that his wife looked after when he was away at sea, and his goats and his fig tree, and the uplands where his goats grazed, where the little wild cyclamen grew among the grass. He spoke English so well that by listening carefully the Players understood almost everything he told them. He was a merry, rather gentle sort of person at most times, with a liking for singing doleful songs about drowned sailormen which made Argos howl in sympathy, as they sat round their supper at the long day's end. But once, when a countryman jostled him rudely in a market crowd, his little bright dagger was out in a flash, and Jonathan had to catch his wrist and tell him not to be a zany and that he wasn't in Genoa now.

It was still drizzling, grey weather when they came down into the fens around Avalon; but the orchards were in blossom, pink and white like sunset clouds, and the marsh-water that lay everywhere reflected back the blossom and the great beds of brown-tufted reeds. Among the fens and the little orchard islands Glastonbury rose like a city in the clouds; and it did not seem quite real even when the Players marched right into it and up the curving narrow streets to the great Pilgrim Inn.

There was a lovely picture of St George killing the dragon, swinging over the courtyard arch; and on the front of the inn were three painted shields: the arms of England in the middle, brilliant in blue and gold and scarlet, and St George's blood-red cross on one side, and on the other a plain white shield with nothing on it at all.

In under the shields and the swinging sign marched the Players, as dusty as any pilgrim that ever came that way. And they stayed three days,

but they did not enact the True and Noble History
of St George. Glastonbury belonged to St George
in a rather special sort of way, but special players
always came to the Pilgrim Inn to act his story
every year, and so it would have been poaching if
Hugh's Players had acted it too.

On the last evening, when they had finished
rehearsing, they were all gathered together in the
small private garden behind the inn, for the inn-
wife, who was a sensible woman and did not think
that being a Strolling Player meant that you were
going to steal the best pewter or dig up the flower-
bulbs, had said that they were welcome to sit in
her garden, it being such a lovely evening. It
really was a lovely evening; grey clouds and
drizzle had cleared away at last, and the sky was
primrose-yellow beyond the gnarled branches of
the apple trees; and the Players and the foreign
sailor sat in a row on a bench before the kitchen
door, with Argos dozing at their feet. It was the
last evening that Paolo would be with them, because they were turning south in the morning, and
he was going on to Bristol; his foot was almost
well again, and he would be able to travel on it
quite well.

'Jonathan,' said Hugh, when they had sat talking lazily for a while, 'could you do something to
my jerkin? It's too tight.'

It certainly was, much too tight. Hugh had
been growing fast since he joined the Company,
and it had been none too big for him in the first
place. Now the sleeves only came half-way down
his arms, and if he did up the buttons, he could
not breathe properly.

' I'll have to put a piece in down the back,' said
Jonathan.   ' 'Twill look a bit odd, I'm afraid.'

' You'd better find a Holy Well and drop pins
down it and ask St George for a new jerkin,' Nicky
told him, breaking off in his efforts to copy a blackbird who was singing most wonderfully in the tallest
apple tree.   ' And while you're about it, you might
ask for one for me, too.   Mine was wore out before
Jasper passed it on to me, and it's very draughty.'

' Wasn't wore out,' protested Jasper, sleepily.
' An' anyway, th' only Holy Well I can think of
hereabouts b'longs to St Bride.   She wouldn't be
int'rested in jerkins.'

Nicky, who had given up trying to imitate the
blackbird, said, ' How do you know she wouldn't? '
simply for the sake of being aggravating.

But before they could really start arguing,
Paolo put in, in his careful English, ' There are,
then, many saints that hava to do with 'ere? '

' Oh yes, Saints in Avalon are as thick as bees in
a lime tree,' said Jonathan.   ' But St George is the
best of the lot.'

' Ah, the St George,' said Paolo.   ' That is his,
the red crossa shield I see above the doorway.'

' That's it,' said Ben Bunsell.   ' How did you
know, you being a foreigner? '

Paolo spread his hands and smiled.   ' Of Genoa
also, St George is the Patron Saint.'

Everybody gazed at him in surprise.   ' But I
say, he's *ours*! ' said Nicky indignantly, and Ben
Bunsell said:

' Then you'll know as much about him as we
do.'

' Ah yes!   'E killa the Dragon,' nodded Paolo.

'That's right,' they said encouragingly.

'And 'e come from the Cappadocia,' said Paolo.

'Don't you b'lieve it,' said Jasper. 'Came from Coventry.'

'Coventry? That is where, please?'

'Somewhere up north—makes knives and buckles and things,' explained Ben. 'If you didn't know that, maybe you don't know about that other shield of his over the doorway—the empty one?'

Paolo shook his head and spread his hands and smiled. 'You will tella me, somebody?'

'Tell him the tale, Jonathan,' said Master Pennifeather.

Jerkins and Holy Wells were forgotten, and everybody settled themselves expectantly. They all knew the story, and they all knew (as most people did in those days, although they have forgotten since) about St George being an Englishman; but they liked to hear Jonathan tell it.

So Jonathan told:

'Well then, St George was the son of a nobleman of Coventry. His mother died when he was but a few hours old, and that same night, while all the castle was in an uproar and full of grief, the babe was stolen out of his cradle with its carved panels and golden bells, by an enchantress called Kalyb. Maybe it was for some spite she had against his father, or maybe she wanted a man-child to rear just for the fun of the thing; or maybe, having the Long Sight, she saw what he would be when he was grown to manhood, and thought she could train him better than his father could do—she having the ancient wisdom and the ancient magic. At all events, out of his cradle she took him, and

carried him away to her own castle and set her
ladies to nurse him; and when he was too old for
their nursing she gave him to her household knights,
to be trained in all the things that a knight should
know. The years went by, and the boy grew tall
and strong, and mastered one by one the many
lessons that he had to learn; and at last the time
came when he was old enough to carry arms.
Then Kalyb gave him a white horse called Bayard,
whose upraised crest and arching mane were like
the crest of a breaking wave; she gave him a plain
white shield, and girded an empty scabbard about
his waist, and she told him: " Go out into the world
and find a sword for your scabbard and a device
for your shield, and I want no more of you, for you
are a man now, and there is no place for you here."
' So St George rode out into the world, and
looked about him for an adventure. But no
adventure befell him until he came riding one evening by the marsh ways into Avalon. There was no
Glastonbury in those days, only a little band of
monks who lived in huts of wattle and daub clustered
together round a wooden hall, like the cells in a
bumble bee's nest; but they gave shelter to travel-
lers, just as the great Abbeys did later on. And
the brown-clad brethren welcomed the young
knight with the blank shield, when he claimed
their hospitality. They stabled his great horse
Bayard, and took him to the guest-hut, and bade
him join them at supper in the long hall. St
George was glad to come to supper, for he was
very hungry, and the coarse brown bread and river-
trout tasted better to him than ever the dainty
fare in Kalyb's castle had done.

'But it seemed to him that the brethren were troubled about something, and when the meal was over, he turned to the old grey Abbot, and said, " Father, it seems to me that there is some trouble upon you all ; if it is so, and there is anything that I can do to help you, I pray you tell me."

' "We are indeed troubled," the Abbot replied, " for we are in danger of losing our greatest treasure, our only treasure."

' " And what is that? And how are you in danger of losing it? "

' " Come with me," said the Abbot, " and I will show it to you."

' And he pushed back his stool, and led the way from the hall, with St George following at his sandalled heels. He led St George to a little hut that was full of golden taper-light, for it was the chapel of the Brotherhood, though 'twas built of wattle and daub, like any shepherd's cot, and the earwigs fell out of the thatch now and then. A young monk who was on guard like a soldier in the doorway stood aside to let them in, and the Abbot pointed silently to a great sword that lay before the altar, with all the glimmering light of the candles on its blade. It was a very plain sword, no damascening on the long, straight blade, no gems enriching the hilt; it was of a strange Eastern design, and so big that only a very tall man could handle it properly, and St George's heart went out to it, and he longed to test its balance and feel the grip in his hand. St George was a tall man.

' " That is your treasure? " he asked.

' " That is our treasure," said the Abbot, and he took it up, handling it as though it were a living thing that he loved. "This is Meribah. With this sword St Peter strove to defend Our Lord, when they came to take Him in the Garden of Gethsemane; and now it is ours, our treasure, and has been these many years. But it seems that it may be ours only a little while longer, for our nearest neighbour—him they call the Raven, from the device on his shield—has sworn to take it from us, and we can do little to withstand him, for he is a powerful knight and we have no champion."

'St George looked again at the great sword, and he said: "I have no sword. If I had, I would be your champion."

' "You shall have Meribah," said the Abbot, his old face brightening with hope. "And if you win your fight, the sword shall be yours to take with you on your way. We would rather die than that Meribah should fall into the hands of such a man as the Raven, but we will give it gladly to a good knight who will keep the blade untarnished and use it to defend the Right," and he put the sword into the young man's eager hands.

'That night St George slept with the sword Meribah against his breast, and the next morning he was sitting cross-legged in the guest-hut doorway, lovingly polishing the blade, when the young monk he had seen the night before in the chapel came scurrying to tell him that the Raven had been seen in the distance, riding that way.

'Up sprang St George, slamming the blade home into his empty sheath, and went with a high heart to saddle Bayard. Bayard was pleased to see him, and whinnied softly when he came in, and slobbered velvety lips on his shoulder while he and the young

monk were saddling and bridling him. But St
George had no time to fondle him just then.
" Presently, Brother Bayard," he promised, " presently you shall have sweet crusts, but now there is
work waiting for us both." And he led the great
horse out into the sunshine where the anxious
monks were waiting, and swung into the saddle.

' Down through the crab-apple and alder trees
rode St George, with his blank shield high on his
shoulder, and the sunlight glancing from helm and
lance-point, and the anxious-eyed brethren in their
brown habits following at Bayard's hairy heels;
down towards the marshland track, where a tall
figure on a black horse was pricking to meet him.
As they drew nearer to each other, St George could
see the raven on the other's shield, and he wished
that his own was not blank and empty. " But
maybe," he thought, " if I win this fight, the Abbot
will give me a device to wear on my shield, as well
as the sword Meribah that he has promised me."
And his heart beat quick and hard, and he could
feel his knightly honour very new and bright inside him, because this was his first fight.

' St George and the Raven came together just
where the track ran through a little flowery meadow,
and St George reined his horse across the way and
bade the other turn back.

' " This is no place for you, messire," said St
George.   " Better go home."

' " And who are you, to tell me so ? " inquired
the Raven, his voice smooth and ugly.

' " I am no one of importance," said St George.
" But I know why you have come, and I tell you
again that you had best go home."

' " Not without the thing I came for," swore the Raven. " What use have these holy men for a sword? If they have any right to it, let them fight for it."

" ' Whatever use they have for it, it is theirs, and none of yours," said St George, touching the hilt. " And I am ready to fight for it on their behalf."

' Then the Raven saw that the weapon at the young knight's side was that same Meribah, and his eyes narrowed as he looked at it. He laughed scornfully. " Go and grow yourself spurs first, my young fighting-cock! You have not even a device to carry on your shield! Give me my sword and go. I do not fight with babes such as you."

' " Do you not? " said St George, gently. " But if you want Meribah, I fear that you must," and he reined Bayard back, and levelled his lance.

' Then the Raven saw that he would indeed have to fight, if he wanted the sword Meribah, and he wheeled his horse away into the far corner of the meadow, and turned with his lance levelled in his hand to face the young knight who had dared to come between him and the thing he wanted. There in the little flowery meadow they fought, while the group of monks huddled against the hedgerow watched them with desperate anxiety. Six times they rode at each other full tilt, and all the meadow grass was churned to mud, but as yet neither of them had gained the mastery. A seventh time they drew back, each to his own end of the meadow, and once again they wheeled their horses and thundered down upon each other. The round clods flew from the horses' hooves, and the air was full of drumming hoof-beats, and the sun flashed back from their armour as they crouched low in their saddles, braced against the shock of the charge. They came together with a ringing crash that seemed to echo across the marshes. The Raven's lance took St George in the left shoulder, and for a moment he swayed in the saddle, with the red blood flowing from his wound in a broad scarlet band down his white shield. Then a groan burst from the little band of watching monks, as he crashed down to the grass. But the Raven had been unhorsed too, and St George was the first to scramble to his feet; and as he did so, they saw that the blood from his wound had flowed across his shield also, and there on its whiteness was a great scarlet cross.

'Both knights drew their swords and rushed upon each other, and for a little while the fight was fast and furious. But St George was growing weak from his wound, and the Raven, seeing this, laughed harshly and began to press him hard, and harder yet. Slowly, St George was forced to give ground, and give ground again; then the Raven swung up his sword for a mighty stroke that would end the battle; but St George gathered the last of his strength and sprang to meet it, with Meribah up-raised. The two blades rang together, and the Raven's sword flew into a score of flashing fragments.

'Now the Raven was at St George's mercy, and he knew it, and flinging the useless hilt from him, stood with folded arms, waiting for Meribah's bright blade to fall again. But St George only leaned wearily on the cross of his sword, and looked at him in a considering sort of way. "You go home now," said St George, breathing short and

They came together with a ringing crash

(See p. 174)

fast, " and don't you go trying to take what doesn't belong to you again, just because the person it does belong to is weaker than you are."

' The Raven bowed his head, and was bitterly ashamed of himself, because St George had spared his life. Then he trailed away to catch his horse, and the brethren, taking no more notice of him than if he had been a beetle, came crowding to St George, who was swaying on his feet, for he had begun to feel as though the little meadow was spinning round him.

' They helped him to mount Bayard and took him back to the guest-hut to have his wound tended, and there he stayed until he was well and strong once more.

' When the time came for him to leave them, the Abbot gave him the sword Meribah to be his own, as he had promised; and St George rode on his way with the sword in his sheath, and the blood-red cross on his white shield that he carried ever afterwards.'

The question of jerkins had been quite forgotten for that evening, but next morning, when the Players were loading up the tilt-cart, Paolo undid his bundle, which they had never seen open before, and brought out from it a doublet of emerald-green velvet, very crumpled and rather threadbare, but strangely and wonderfully enriched with tarnished silver lace and knots of tinsel ribbon.

It was the kind of doublet that made you blink to look at it, and the Players blinked, as Paolo held it up at arm's length. ' I am not the St George, that you drop pins down my 'Oly Well,' said Paolo. ' But I give the doublet all the same, to Nicky, and to Hugh. It may be a little too large, but they will grow to it.'

The Players, who had all gathered round to gaze admiringly, said: 'Oh, but you can't possibly want to give *that* away,' and 'What would you do without it, yourself?' But Hugh and Nicky only looked longingly at the green doublet in hopeful silence.

'For me, it is too brave,' said Paolo, shaking out the creases. 'It was give to me by a grand Signor 'oo come the voyage long, long time ago. 'E was ver' sick, that Signor; I am kind to 'im, and 'e love me like a brother. When 'e is no more sick, 'e no more love me like a brother, but 'e do not take back the doublet. Now I give it to you.'

'Well, if you're sure,' said Hugh and Nicky in one breath. 'It's *very* good of you.'

'For me, the poor sailor, it is too grand; also it is a little tight; but for you, the so-great Players, it is justa the thing,' Paolo assured them, and gave the precious doublet into their hands.

'I shall wear it first because I'm the eldest,' said Nicky. 'You can have it to-morrow, Dusty.' And then and there, while the others went back to loading the tilt-cart, he stripped off his ragged jerkin and put on the wonderful green doublet. It was not so very much too large, after all, and he swaggered across to join the others with as much of an air as Captain Raleigh himself. 'How do I look?' demanded Nicky, preening himself and trying to see his own back.

'You look,' said Jasper Nye, 'like a moulting yaffle.'

Luckily Paolo did not know what moulting

meant, or that a yaffle was a green woodpecker, and so his feelings were not ruffled; and as Nicky was quite sure that he looked simply splendid in the green doublet and Jasper was only jealous, *his* feelings were not ruffled either; and he set to work with a will to help Jonathan harness Saffronilla.

When all was ready, they said good-bye to Paolo, and thanked him again for his present, and wished him fair winds and good fortune, and set out.

The last they saw of the foreign sailor, he was standing in the archway of the inn-yard, under the great swing-sign of St George killing the dragon. He flung up his arm and called something after them. They didn't know what, because it was in Italian, but it had a friendly sound. So they waved and called back. Then they went on down the street, and the houses hid him from sight, and soon they were among the orchards again, with their faces turned towards the south.

There was a little wind that day, scattering the apple-blossom from the trees, and Hugh, trudging along beside Jonathan as usual, kept his eye on that wonderful flame-green doublet going on before through the drifting petals, and thought pleasantly about it being his turn to wear it to-morrow.

' Funny about St George and that green doublet,' he said to Jonathan. ' Nice, too.'

But he never guessed how very nearly his half of Paolo's gift was going to bring disaster upon him !

XI

UNCLE JACOB

THEY reached Exeter in the full flush of May. Hawthorn whitened the hedges and the first cuckoos were calling; lady's-smock a-dance in the meadows, and the squat grey towers of the Cathedral rising from a green froth of trees in new leaf.

Hugh's pot of periwinkle, carefully nursed and shielded all through the winter, was gay with blue flowers again, and the people in the south Devon villages had flocked in to see the Players, so that there was supper *and* breakfast *and* warm stables to sleep in, day after day and night after night, and life was very good. It went on being good when they got to Exeter. The Mayor seemed really pleased when they asked him for a licence (Mayors were often not at all pleased, even when they gave the licence). And the Players encamped at the Black Lion, and decided to stay three days, which was the longest they ever stopped anywhere.

On the first day they enacted the Martyrdom of St Sebastian. On the second day they acted a new play which Jonathan had made from an old story about Sir Huon of Bordeaux, who accidentally killed one of Charlemagne's knights, and got mixed up in a great many difficult and exciting adventures in consequence, and finished up by disappearing into Fairyland with the Emir of Babylon's daughter. On the third day they per-

formed the True and Noble History of St George,
which Hugh liked the best of all their plays, because
it was the first he had ever seen. Hugh played the
King of Egypt's daughter now, while Nicky was
only the Populace, because Nicky's voice was
breaking, and so he was playing parts that didn't
need much talking, just then. Hugh had grown
out of the yellow satin farthingale as well as his
own jerkin, and Jonathan had let it down, with a
band of ruby-coloured velvet round the hem,
which everyone thought was an improvement.

All three plays were a great success, but St George
was the greatest success of all. There were a lot
of extra people in Exeter, because of a great Wool
Fair that was being held, and most of them seemed
to have come to see St George. The courtyard
was packed with them. They bulged through the
carved rails of the gallery and hung over the balustrade leading up to it, and craned their necks out
of windows, shouting and yelling most joyously all
the while the fight was raging between St George
and the dragon, so that really it was a wonder
they did not have the Watch on them, to see what
all the noise was about.

When the performance was over, and the crowd
had melted away, the Players began to repack the
costume baskets, ready to take the road in the
morning. And that was when Argos got bored and
wandered out through the archway into the street.
Hugh dropped the King's mantle he had been
folding and ran out too, to fetch him back before he
got kicked by a passing horse or run over by a dray,
because it was a very busy street, and Argos was
not clever about traffic. He grabbed Argos from

the middle of the crowded way and hauled him back into the inn archway; and then a string of pack-horses came by from the Wool Fair, with bells jingling on their harness and ornaments of blue and scarlet worsted on their ears and across their breasts, and he waited to watch them pass.

And just as the last one went by, he saw Uncle Jacob!

He had never for one moment thought of being afraid of meeting Uncle Jacob so far from his own farm as Exeter, nor had the rest of the Company, or they would never have taken Hugh over the Devon border. But the Wool Fair must have brought him, as it had brought so many others from their distant farms, and there he was, at the corner of the street, and at the same instant that Hugh saw him, he saw Hugh! It was Hugh's turn to wear the wonderful green doublet, and it was the brilliance of it, glistening in the sunlight, that had caught Uncle Jacob's eye. If it hadn't been for that doublet, Uncle Jacob might never have seen him at all, for the corner of the street was quite a long way from the archway of the Black Lion; but it was too late to think of that now. Just for an instant everything seemed to go very still and queer, like a bad dream, and Hugh's heart began to thump high in his throat, like the heart of a rabbit with a stoat after it, so that it made him feel sick.

Then, as Uncle Jacob began to shoulder through the crowd towards him, he whirled round, grabbed Argos by the collar, and made for the open door of the stable where his friends were, dragging the huge dog with him. He reached the door, shot through and slammed it behind him, and stood panting with his back to it, as the others looked up inquiringly.

'Jonathan! It's Uncle Jacob!' he gasped. 'He's seen me—don't let him get Argos!'

Nobody wasted an instant in being surprised and wondering what Uncle Jacob was doing in Exeter, because being rogues and vagabonds had taught them not to waste time in an emergency.

'Did he see Argos?' demanded Master Pennifeather, as they all sprang to their feet.

Hugh shook his head.

'Then he can't be sure of you. You've changed since he saw you last. Did he see you come in here—to this door, I mean?'

Hugh shook his head again. He couldn't speak, because his mouth felt so dry.

'Then he'll have gone to the house-door first. Take off that doublet.' Master Pennifeather began issuing orders like a general, while Benjamin tore Hugh out of the green doublet. 'Jonathan, go and head him off for five minutes, and we'll make him think Jasper's got the plague; that should get rid of him. Nicky, get into that doublet; Jasper, the black jerkin out of the small basket—I want it quickly!—Dusty, it's the hay-loft for you, my hero.'

Before Hugh quite knew what was happening, he had been punted over the edge of the half-floor of the hay-loft, and Argos had been heaved up beside him, and Jonathan had gone out, closing the stable door again.

'Don't worry,' said Master Pennifeather, grinning up at him and already shrugging himself into

the black jerkin. 'Get well back from the edge
and keep Argos quiet, and your uncle shan't get
either of you. He shan't, anyway, because if the
worst comes to the worst, we'll put him in the horse-
trough, but we'll try what the plague will do first.'

And he turned away to issue a great many orders
to the rest of the Company.

Hugh crept back into the shadows, and crouched
down against the farthest wall, with his arms so
tight round Argos's neck to keep him quiet, that
the dog was all but throttled. There they stayed,
as still as though they were shadows themselves,
except that they were both shivering a little, and
shadows do not shiver.

Meanwhile Jonathan was strolling across the
yard towards a stout and angry man who was
talking loudly to a serving-maid in the inn doorway.

'Yiss, there's a young boy with 'em, for sure,' the
maid was saying. '*And* a' wears a green doublet.
See'd un' in it just now, I did.' And then she saw
Jonathan. 'There's one o' the Players coming
across the yard now. You'd better ask him,
maister.'

The stout man swung round on Jonathan, and
demanded, 'Where be my nephew?'

'Your nephew?' said Jonathan, slowly. 'Do I
know your nephew?'

'The boy—the boy in the green doublet,' splut-
tered the angry farmer. ''Tisn't no manner of
good your telling me you bain't got a boy in a green
doublet.'

Jonathan looked at him in a puzzled fashion,
and then smiled pleasantly. 'Oh, you'll be mean-

ing Nicky Bodkyn,' he said. 'I never knew he had an uncle. Never knew he had a father or mother, for that matter. We found him sitting in the stocks at Romsey, for stealing eggs.'

The farmer looked surprised for a moment. Then he said more politely, 'If 'tis as I suspicion, you've been deceived in that lad; he's my nephew Hugh. Ran away from a good home, a' did, 'bout a year ago, and took a valuable dog with him.'

Jonathan remembered what Hugh had told him about the good home, and he thought he should very much like to rub Uncle Jacob's nose on the cobbles, but he went on smiling pleasantly, and shook his head. 'I'm afraid it is not as you suspicion, master; Nicky has been with us four years or more.'

'How do I know that?' demanded Uncle Jacob.

Jonathan sighed and shrugged. 'You have only my word for it, but it is perfectly true.'

But Uncle Jacob did not believe him, and he rattled his stick on the cobbles, and said, 'Now I tell 'ee what 'tis, young man. You'm hiding something from me. I demand to see that boy of yours.'

'All in good time,' said Jonathan, propping himself against the hitching-post. 'I am not your dog, that I should run to do your bidding with my tail a-wag behind me, and I'll thank you to remember that, master.'

Then Uncle Jacob began to shout. 'Who are you to talk like that to a respectable farmer, you ugly, long-armed, thieving vagabond.'

Jonathan flushed under his tan, and his eyes

grew very bright, but he answered slowly and easily, 'If I am a thieving vagabond, my respectable friend, look out for your wallet. As to my being ugly, I freely admit it; but how much better to be intelligent than beautiful. Do you not feel that yourself, sir? And if my arms are long, that is quite a useful thing, when the fists at the end of them are hard. Oh, but have no fear, I wouldn't clench them against an old grey-headed man like you, because I was nicely brought up. See, I'm as gentle as a kitten . . .' and he waggled his thumbs under Uncle Jacob's nose in the most insulting manner.

He had to gain time somehow, and being aggravating and fantastical seemed quite a good way of doing it (and one good thing about being a Player was that you could be as fantastical as you liked, without anyone thinking it at all suspicious). But Uncle Jacob was one of those people who have only one idea at a time, and his idea just then was to have another look at the boy in the green doublet who he had glimpsed for a moment in the archway, and find out whether or not it really *was* Hugh. So he tried to brush past the Player; and Jonathan had to stop waggling his thumbs and think of some other way of delaying him.

'I shouldn't be in too great a hurry to come to close quarters with our Company, if I were you,' he said. 'One of our lads was taken sick after the performance, and we do not yet know what it is—but we're afraid of the Plague.'

That did make Uncle Jacob stop to think; because in those days, if people were taken ill suddenly, it quite likely *might* be the Plague—or the

H

sweating-sickness, which was almost as bad. Still, he was not at all sure that the Player was telling him the truth, and the boy in the green doublet had certainly been very like Hugh. So he said more politely, 'Still, I'll take a look inside that stable you've come out of—I reckon that's where he is.'

'Yes, all of us,' said Jonathan. 'Come and look, if you wish.' (Surely they had had all the time they needed, in there!) And he turned and lounged back towards the stable door, with Uncle Jacob fretting and fuming beside him. At the door he halted again, and asked tenderly, 'Are you sure you want to risk catching it?'

'I don't believe there's anything to catch,' said Uncle Jacob.

He did not say it very certainly, but still, Jonathan knew that if he put him off any longer, the man would begin to suspect that he was playing for time. So he raised the latch with a loud rattle, and flung the door open.

Uncle Jacob stood on the threshold and stared. Evidently the Player *had* spoken the truth, after all.

In the farther shadows of the big stall stood a square man with a peacock's feather in his bonnet and a perfectly strange boy in a green doublet, both staring anxiously at a third, who lay on a pile of straw against one wall, looking very ill indeed. The man on the straw moved his head restlessly from side to side, his eyes were half closed and he breathed short and fast. A respectable-looking man in black was kneeling beside him with his back to the door.

Now, if Aunt Alison had been there she would

Looking very ill indeed

(See p. 186)

very likely have seen through the whole plot, because she was a great deal cleverer than Uncle Jacob, as well as being a great deal nastier. But she was at home looking after the farm, and Uncle Jacob simply went on staring, and never guessed that in the hay-loft overhead, Hugh and Argos were staring too—staring down through mounds of heaped-up hay with their four eyes nearly strained out of their heads. Poor Argos was shuddering all over, with his tail between his legs, because he knew who was below; and Hugh was clutching him round the neck and trying to stop him being afraid, which was not easy because he was so desperately afraid himself.

'You see?' said Jonathan, in a low voice, and then turned to the respectable-looking man in black. 'What is it, doctor?'

The doctor raised his head slowly, and got up. 'It is the sweating-sickness,' he said. 'It is earlier than usual in the City this year. There are a great many cases of it about.'

'What are we to do for him?' asked Jonathan.

'Keep him quiet, and keep the door open. I will send you some medicine, but——' The doctor shook his head doubtfully, and went to pick up his hat, moving heavily, as though he was tired out with overwork.

Jonathan turned to Uncle Jacob, who was still staring as though his eyes were never going to come properly back into his head again, and said, 'If I were you, I should go away quickly, master— very quickly indeed.'

'I *will*!' said Uncle Jacob, feelingly, and backed away. 'I'll be going this moment. Sorry to have troubled you, I'm sure!' And he lumbered out of the courtyard very fast indeed, with the fear of the terrible sweating-sickness showing clearly all over his broad back.

Jonathan and the doctor (who of course was Master Pennifeather) watched him go in silence, and when he was gone they shut the door very firmly.

'That's all right, then,' said Master Pennifeather. 'The only danger was that he might meet one of the inn people and tell them we had the sickness, but he hasn't.'

Jasper got up off the straw and stretched in a languid sort of way; and Nicky sat down in his green doublet, and buried his face, which had suddenly turned scarlet, on his knees, and laughed so that his shoulders shook.

'He deserved the fright of his life, and he's got it,' said Benjamin happily. 'He'll be looking for spots on his chest for a good many nights to come.'

'It's all right now. You can come down, Dusty,' said Jonathan, and held up his long arms to catch him as he scrambled down.

Argos jumped down after him, making the 'wumph!' sort of noise that a big dog generally makes when he jumps off something high.

'Gentlemen,' said Master Pennifeather, beginning to unfasten the black jerkin, 'I congratulate you! I congratulate *me*! We have just given the most superb performance of our lives!'

Then his eye fell on Nicky, still spluttering and rocking, and he began to laugh too, and Ben and Jasper joined in. They laughed in the way that people only laugh a few times in all their lives, first clinging to the hay-racks and each other, then sitting on the floor with their legs stuck straight out in front of them and the tears hopping down their crimson faces; laughed at last draped across the costume baskets, snatching at their breath and crowing as though they had the whooping cough even if they hadn't got the sweating-sickness.

Only Hugh and Jonathan did not laugh. They stood and looked at each other, while Argos whimpered and shuddered against Hugh's legs. Jonathan was smiling in his queer winged way, but there was a grey look at the corners of his mouth.

When the others were beginning to sit up and wipe their eyes on the backs of their hands, Ben Bunsell said, ' That was a noble lie of yours, Toby, to tell him Exeter was full of the sweating-sickness! I'd wager my boots, if they were worth the wagering, that he'll have gone straight off to collect his horse, and he'll not stop until he's ten good miles on his homeward way! '

' It is my sincere and pious hope that you are right,' said Master Pennifeather. ' But all the same, I think 'twould be as well if we took the road to-night, my lords, instead of waiting till the morning.'

So they did. Everything was ready packed, and in the blue spring twilight the Company made their way out of Exeter, by narrow, winding streets where the overhanging upper storeys of the houses on either side almost touched the top of the tilt as the little cart trundled by.

All the meadows were awash with dusk when they came out into open country. The first owls were hooting, and the scent of hawthorn was thick and sweet on the quiet air; and when Hugh turned to look back, the sky was fading pink above the lights that were pricking out in the old city.

Hugh and Jonathan were walking a little behind the others, as usual, and suddenly Hugh said in a small hot rush: 'I heard what Uncle Jacob shouted at you—right through the hay-loft wall, I heard it. He—he *insulted* you, and it was all because of me!'

Jonathan gave his shoulder a friendly shake. 'You'll have had a good many worse things than that shouted at you, by the time you've been a Strolling Player as long as I have,' he said. 'Don't be a zany, Brother Dusty-Feet. Anyhow, what does it matter, on an evening like this, with streets and houses left behind you, and the white road ahead, and the fern and the hawthorn smelling? And there'll be a new moon presently.'

So Hugh felt better.

They found a nice place to sleep, in the corner of a spinney, with soft springing fern to lie on, and a little stream running by to sing them all through the quiet spring night and for watering Saffronilla. And Hugh lay curled up like a dormouse between Argos and Jonathan. They were all three very happy.

XII

WHITE HART FOREST

BACK they went into Dorset once more, and Hugh was a little sad at first, because people who belong to the West Country always leave a bit of their heart behind them, if they go eastward. But after all, they were heading more or less towards Oxford once again, and though his old home was behind him, the dream beckoned from far ahead, as it always did when his feet were turned in that direction; and after a while he began to feel happier. And by the time they turned away from the direction of Oxford and came down into Blackmoor Vale he had got over leaving the West Country; so he went on being happy. Besides, Blackmoor Vale was lovely.

Jonathan said it used to be called White Hart Forest, because of a wonderful white hart that King Henry III had found when he was hunting in the forest there. It had been so beautiful—a snow-white hart standing at bay amongst the green leaves—that the King had called off his hounds and let it go; and the Vale had been called after it almost ever since. Very likely it was a fairy hart, Jonathan said; the Vale was one of those places where things happen that don't happen in everyday places.

After a few days they decided to go to Sherborne. It was late July by that time, and the foxgloves and the dog-roses were almost over; but the honeysuckle still blew its golden trumpets along every hedge-top, and the lanes were deep in meadowsweet smelling like honey, and the meadows were spread with a golden carpet of buttercups in which the stately trees and sleepy cows stood knee deep. It had been a grey rainy morning as the Company took the Sherborne road, but after they had eaten their midday bread-and-cheese in the shelter of a horse-chestnut tree that let heavy cold drops through on to their heads or down their necks when they least expected it, it began to clear up, and by evening the raindrops clinging to every leaf and petal were sparkling like diamonds, the small birds had begun to sing, and all the world was golden. The puddles in the rutted lane were golden-ruffled at the edges, and the buttercups powdering the meadows were like a fairy carpet spread for Sir Huon of Bordeaux; even the clouds that were piled up far ahead of them had golden crests, though they were grey and lavender underneath, and the great tower of the Abbey rising in the distance above the warm roofs of Sherborne was more golden than all beside.

Just outside the town the Company halted as usual, to get out the drum and sackbut, and then marched on again in triumphal style, legs straight and heads up, swaggering along to the rub-a-dub and tran-ta-ran of the drum and sackbut, as proud as a Sovereign's escort or a peacock with three tails.

Up the winding main street they went, between tall, gabled houses with lovely oriel windows jutting out above their heads, past the great golden Abbey, where the pigeons crooned and fluttered among the pinnacles, and down another street to the Sun Inn, where they meant to stay three days.

The Sun Inn was golden too, like the Abbey, and so near to it that when you stood beside the horse-trough in the courtyard you could see the top of the tower over the inn roof. That was just as it should be, because in an odd way the inn seemed to belong to the Abbey—rather in the same way that a solid and loyal squire might belong to a tall and stately knight. It seemed to have been built out of the same stuff as the Abbey, too, and it had a gargoyle just like one of those in the Abbey, above the stable arch; a nice gargoyle with a friendly, laughing face like a faun's, which Hugh liked from the first moment he saw it, even more than the lovely long-winged angel in a niche over the house doorway.

Later that evening, after Master Pennifeather had called upon the Mayor, and they had proclaimed to the town that they were going to play the Martyrdom of St Cecilia (whose costumes had been mended long since) at four o'clock next afternoon, and had their supper in the crowded, cheerful common room of the inn, they all sat side by side along the edge of the huge stone horse-trough in the twilight, taking their ease for a little while before beginning the nightly rehearsal. Behind them in the inn there was firelight and candle-light and a babble of voices, and somebody began to sing in a loud, merry voice:

'Would you hear a Spanish Lady,
How she wooed an Englishman?
Garments gay and rich as may be,
Decked with jewels she had on.'

But out in the courtyard it was cool and quiet, and the after-glow was the colour of evening primroses behind the blotty darkness of the gabled inn roof and the Abbey tower that seemed to stand a-tiptoe to reach up towards the first star. Suddenly a bell began to ring, high up in the lacy tower, lovely, slow, golden notes stealing out and dropping into the courtyard of the Sun Inn, so that Hugh felt that if he put up his hands he would be able to catch one—like a golden bubble.

' That's the curfew,' said Master Pennifeather.

' That's Great Tom,' said Jonathan; and he told Hugh how Cardinal Wolsey had given it to be the great tenor bell of Sherborne Abbey, in the days when he was the most powerful man in England, and how it took six men to ring it.

> ' By Wolsey's gift I measure time for all.
> To Mirth, to Grief, to Church I serve to call.'

' That is what is written on its side,' said Jonathan. ' But folks came to the Abbey a goodish long while before Wolsey's bell called them.'

' How long? ' asked Hugh.

Jonathan turned his face to him in the dusk, and said: ' More than eight hundred years, Dusty. But 'twas only a little Saxon Cathedral church then; and St Aldhelm built it and was its first bishop.'

Hugh swung his heels contentedly against the side of the horse-trough, hoping for a story. ' Tell about St Aldhelm,' he said. ' What did he do to be made a saint? '

' He did a hard job of work, and did it well,' said Jonathan. ' It was before the Normans came, you

know—long before—and in those days people didn't
get made into saints for seeing visions, as they did
later, but for doing a good job of work, with perhaps a vision or two thrown in. Well, St Aldhelm
was a monk. Monks didn't stay shut away from
the world within high walls then, as they were
doing when King Hal broke up the Monasteries—
they went out and told people about God and how
to get the best out of their crops, and tried to stop
them putting dung on their sore places and knock-
ing on the head people whom they didn't like.
That was what St Aldhelm did. He was a brown
man, they say, with a deep, strong singing voice,
and he could sing the songs of the countryside, just
as well as he could sing the offices of the Church.
There wasn't a minstrel in the South Country,
they say, to equal St Aldhelm; just plain Aldhelm
he was, in those days, of course—a young monk of
no importance. And when he was sent out to
preach to the people, he would take up his place
where there were a great many people coming and
going, such as a bridge or a market square, and
sing the songs of the minstrel-folk until he had
gathered his crowd, and perhaps for a little while
afterwards, for he loved singing. He would then
lay aside his harp and tell them about God.'

Jasper Nye made a disapproving sort of noise in
his throat, as though he didn't think a monk
ought to sing minstrel songs to gather the people
he was going to preach to; and Nicky said, ' Didn't
his Abbot *mind*? '

' No,' said Jonathan, and though Hugh could
not see his face clearly, he knew that he was smiling,
by the sound of his voice. ' The Abbot was a wise

man, who knew that if it is good to carve in stone
or make church music or paint in azure and ver-
milion to the Glory of God, it is just as good to
juggle with coloured balls or sing minstrel songs to
the Glory of God, if you do that better. So Aldhelm was left to gather his crowds in his own way.

'The years went by, and Aldhelm became an
Abbot himself—Abbot of Malmesbury—and he did
not go out singing and preaching any more, because
he had too many other things to do.

'And more years went by, and Aldhelm grew
old. Then one day King Ina of Wessex sent for
him to Winchester, which was the capital in those
days; and that night they ate the evening meal
together in the King's Great Hall, among his house-
thegns and with his hunting-dogs crouching under
the table for scraps.

'And afterwards, as they sat comfortably over
their ale-horn, the King said to Aldhelm, "Aldhelm, you know that I have made a new Bishopric
of Sherborne?"

'And Aldhelm said, "Yes, and a very unruly
Bishopric it is, if all I hear be true."

'"It is quite true," said Ina. "The people are
a stiff-necked crew, from the richest thegn to the
poorest serf, and many of them hold to the old
gods, with all the faith and loyalty that is in them."

'"And for that very reason, they are the more
worth winning over," said Aldhelm. "For the
more stubbornly a man keeps faith once, the more
likely he is to keep faith again. Besides, that sort
makes the best fighting men," said he. "And I
ever loved a good fighting man."

'Ina leaned forward across the table to look at

the Abbot, with his chin cupped between his fists. "You're something of a fighting man yourself, in your own way, I reckon," says he. "How would you like to fight Thor and Odin in the Bishopric of Sherborne?" (Thor and Odin were the old gods.)

'Aldhelm didn't answer at once, and Ina pressed him eagerly. "Well—will you be the first Bishop of Sherborne?"

'Still Aldhelm went on thinking. He was an old man, and tired; he thought of his great Abbey of Malmesbury, the shady cloisters and the quiet life, the peach trees in the high-walled garden; and the part of him that was old and tired longed to go back there and end his days in peace; but another part of him was eager for the fight and the adventure. "Aye," he said, "I'll do it." And he went out from the King's Hall, Bishop of Sherborne.

'But he did not go with his mitre on his head and his crozier in his hand, to take possession of his bishopric. Instead he put on the gay, shabby clothes of a wandering minstrel, and set out, carrying his harp. It was just as it had been when he was young, you see. Many years had gone by since he sang in the market-places, but he had not lost the knack, and he could still charm the heart out of those who heard him. So for a long while he lived the life of a strolling minstrel, up and down his bishopric, singing in the houses of Christian and Pagan alike. If people asked him who he was, he told them, otherwise he never spoke of it. Folks thought he was crazed, of course; a Bishop strolling up and down the countryside, singing the songs of the ordinary folk and the deeds of ancient

heroes; but they liked his songs and they liked
him, and they welcomed the Minstrel in to sit by
their fire and eat at their table—those stiff-necked
thegns, and the poor folk too—when they wouldn't
have let the Bishop across the door-sill. So little
by little, he won their trust and friendship, and
when the time was ripe for it, he began to build his
church. . . .

'And people said, "Well, he do sing a master-
fine song, to be sure. Us'll go and hear if he can
preach as fine a sermon." So they went.

'It was only a little church, that first one; no
tall tower, no Great Tom. I think St Aldhelm
would have liked Great Tom for his splendid voice;
there would have been a fellow-feeling betwixt those
two.'

For a while nobody said anything, and then
Hugh said, 'You know a tremendous lot about
the Abbey and the Vale, don't you?'

And Jonathan said, 'Why, you see, all this
country is home to me. I was born and bred up
yonder towards Bulbarrow Down.'

Hugh looked round at him in surprise. Somehow he had never thought of Jonathan being born
and bred anywhere, only of being Jonathan, the
Strolling Player; and he wondered suddenly about
Jonathan's home, and why he had left it, and if
perhaps he would go back one day. If they had
been alone, he might have asked, but they were
not, and anyway there was no time, for at that
moment Master Pennifeather got up and stretched
until the small muscles cracked behind his shoulders.
'Time we were at our rehearsing,' he said. 'You've
not the least notion how to play that tavern scene,

Ben, and you'll get it right before we seek our couches for the night, if I have to break your neck *and* my own, to teach you.'

On their second day in Sherborne the Company acted the play about Sir Huon of Bordeaux, which was a particularly nice one, really, funny in places and exciting in other places, with a lot of magic in it, and a happy ending. Most of the plays about saints ended sadly, so it made a nice change. Hugh played Esclaremond, the Emir of Babylon's daughter, in a green kirtle with hanging sleeves of rose-pink taffeta, and a wig of long golden hair. The kirtle had a long rent in the skirt where Hugh had caught it on a nail, but Jonathan (who played Oberon the Fairy King, in scarlet tights, with a fantastic crown instead of the horns that usually went with them) had mended it so that it was as good as new. It was the most lovely colour, like the deep moss that grows under beech trees.

When they were changing for the performance, and more and more people were arriving every moment, Jasper Nye found that he had got the wrong stockings; brown when they should have been purple. So Hugh, who was still in his ordinary clothes, because Esclaremond did not appear until quite late in the play, was sent across to the stable where the costume baskets were, to fetch the right ones. It took Hugh rather a long time to find the purple stockings, because Argos was being helpful, as usual; and by the time he came out into the courtyard again it was as full as ever it could be. There were craftsmen and prentices, farm folk from the country round with soil caked on their boots, and merchant folk and gentlefolk, and lads from Sherborne School, who were not really supposed to be there at all, and a horse being edged through the crowd (that was one of the draw-backs of acting in inn-yards—horses having to be got in and out). It was a most glorious crush, people jostling and pushing and craning their necks for a better view, and the sunshine slanting down on all the colours of a summer flower-plot mingling and swaying together as the throng shifted, and in the midst of it all, the rush-strewn stage, empty and waiting.

Hugh dived into the crowd and began to butt and edge and sidle his way through, with Argos at his heels. He was close under one of the crowded galleries when he heard a small, imperious voice above his head, calling, 'Hi! Boy!—Boy-boy-boy!'

He stopped so suddenly that Argos bumped into him from behind, and looked up; and there, hanging so far over the carved gallery rail that she looked as if she might come down into the court-yard on her head at any moment, was a little girl. Just for a moment Hugh thought she might be a Pharisee, because she looked like one; a small brown sparkling Pharisee in a leaf-green kirtle. But then he saw that there was a tall brown man just behind her, who was laughing, with a hand twisted in the back folds of her skirt to make sure she did not fall on her head; and no one would do that to the Fairy-kind, because it would be dis-respectful.

'Boy,' said the little girl, 'are you in the play?'

'Yes, little mistress,' said Hugh, 'I'm the heroine.'

Then somebody bumped into him, and he remembered Jasper waiting for his purple stockings, and went butting on through the crowd to the dim little room behind the stage, without ever noticing that the brown man had bent forward quickly, and was looking after him, rather as though he thought he knew him and wanted to make sure.

Hugh thought about the little girl and the brown man all the time he was putting on Esclaremond's green kirtle and yellow wig; and he went on thinking about them while he sat on his heels, listening to the others on the stage outside and waiting until it was time to join them. And when at last he climbed on to the stage, gathering the folds of his kirtle elegantly in one hand and carrying a white clove carnation in the other, he saw that the little girl was still hanging over the gallery rail. She waved to him, but of course he couldn't wave back, and she looked dreadfully hurt until a lady standing beside her bent down to whisper in her ear; and then she understood, and stopped looking hurt.

As the play went on, Hugh had quite a lot of chances to glance at the little girl and her family, and the more he glanced at them, the nicer they seemed. There were four of them, and you could tell that they *were* a family, because they had the look of people who belong together. The little girl had just the starry look that wind-flowers have, only that wind-flowers look as though they could not be naughty if they tried, and the little girl looked as though she could be very naughty indeed without having to try at all. The brown man, who must

She waved to him

(See p. 202)

be her father, had eyes that crinkled up into dancing slits, in the nicest way, when they came to the funny bits of the play; and the lady, who must be her Mammy, looked as though she would smell nice—of clove carnations, perhaps, or some other flower whose smell was warm and cosy. There was a boy, too; a dark boy in a crimson doublet, a bit older than Hugh, who looked just the sort of person it would be nice to have adventures with.

There were so many, many people in the courtyard, but those four stood out from among them all, or at least it seemed to Hugh that they did; and he wished and *wished* that he knew them.

When the play was over, and the Players had changed back into their dusty workaday clothes and come out into the yard again, and all the people were gone, Hugh felt quite forlorn for a moment, because the family had gone too, and the big courtyard seemed very empty without them. Quite suddenly he thought how nice it would be to have a family of his own. Then Jonathan turned in the inn doorway below the long-winged angel, and called to him; and he forgot about not having a family, because having Jonathan was just as good, and they went in to their supper together.

XIII

THE PARTING OF THE WAYS

THE next evening the brown man with the crinkly eyes was in the gallery again, and the boy was with him, but not the little girl or her mother. All through the play the man watched Hugh very closely—leaning forward with his brown hands on the carved rail—in a way that made him feel prickly up the back of his neck. And afterwards, when they were changing, Will the stable-man suddenly appeared in the doorway, looking very disapproving (he didn't like nasty dirty Players all over his nice clean stable) and said, ' I wants the young 'un. He'm to come with me d'rectly.'

Everybody looked at Hugh, and then at each other, and Jonathan asked, ' What do you want him for?'

' 'Tisn't me as wants him,' said the stable-man, with a sniff. ' Gentleman in the Mistress's garden wants him most particular; don't ask me *why*.'

Suddenly Hugh had the queerest feeling inside, a kind of tingling ' something-is-going-to-happen ' feeling; and he didn't want to go. But Jonathan punted him gently towards the door.

' Go along with you, Dusty,' he said.

And Hugh went. The surly stable-man grabbed the back of his neck-band, and marched him across the yard rather as though he was a beadle and Hugh was under arrest, and thrust him in through the inn doorway.

'Yere 'ee be, Missis,' said the man, while Hugh
rubbed the back of his neck and glared.

Then the mistress of the house, who was large
and billowy and much kinder than her stable-man,
bounced out from an inner room, and said, 'Dear
heart alive! What have you been doing to the
child? Here, pull your neck-band straight, my
chuck, it's half-way down your back. That's right.
Now come along with me. Mr Heritage is in my
private garden.'

Mr Heritage! That was the name of the friend
his father had served at Oxford! Hugh felt as
though he must be dreaming and would wake up
at any moment. 'Here! mistress!' he gasped, as
they scurried along through the crowded common
room into the family's private rooms beyond. 'Is
it—Mr Anthony Heritage?'

'Aye, that's him, Mr Anthony Heritage from
Prior's Caundle,' said the inn-wife, and she opened
yet another door, and pushed Hugh out into a long,
narrow strip of garden between high yew hedges,
and shut the door behind him with a determined
little slam.

It was a nice garden, with a straight strip of
camomile lawn like a green riband leading down
it instead of a path, and on either side a lovely drift
of snap-dragon and sweet-smelling yellow musk all
humming with brown velvet bees. Right at the
far end was a shady green vine-arbour; and in the
arbour sat the crinkly-eyed man and the dark boy
who looked as if he would be nice to have adventures
with.

They got up when they saw Hugh, and stood
waiting for him. They both looked very clean;

their ruffs were crisp and fresh and their doublets
fitted them beautifully; and as he looked at them,
Hugh felt how brown and dusty he was, and how
patched and ragged his clothes were, and how his
shoes were stuffed with rags because their soles were
worn out. But he couldn't keep Mr Heritage
waiting; so he pushed back his shoulders and
straightened his legs as the Players had taught him,
and marched down the green riband to the arbour.

'You sent for me, sir,' he said.

The man said, 'Yes, I sent for you.' And he
put his hands on Hugh's shoulders, and looked down
at him, very searchingly, but so kindly that Hugh
forgot about his dust and the holes in his shoes.
'What is your name?' asked the brown man.

'Hugh,' said Hugh. 'Hugh Copplestone.'

'I thought so,' said the man. 'You're very like
your father. Mine is Anthony Heritage.'

'The inn-wife told me that,' said Hugh.

'Have you ever heard my name before?'

Hugh nodded. 'My father used to talk about
you often. He was your servitor at Oriel.'

Mr Heritage sat down again, and looked at him
without a trace of his crinkly smile. 'And how
comes Peter Copplestone's son to be trapesing about
the country with a band of Strolling Players?'

Hugh took a deep breath and explained—about
his father having died, and about Aunt Alison,
and about Argos. 'And I couldn't let her have
Argos knocked on the head; so we ran away.'

'Bravo!' said the dark boy, who had stood quite
still all this while. 'Oh, bravo, Hugh!'

'And we hadn't got any friends, or anywhere to
go, so I thought we'd go to Oxford. Father used to

tell me about Oxford, and Master Bodley's lectures and—and everything; he always meant me to go to Oriel; he said we'd manage somehow. So I thought if we went to Oxford, perhaps we'd make our fortunes somehow; and then on the second day we met Master Pennifeather and the others, and they took us on with them.'

'I see.' Mr Heritage stuck his arms akimbo, and watched one of the Abbey pigeons flying overhead with the evening sunlight under its wings. 'Poor old Peter! I wish I'd kept in touch with him,' he said in a raw, regretful voice. Then he stopped watching the pigeon, and looked down at Hugh again. 'My son Martin, here, is just home from Oriel for the summer holidays,' he said. 'When he goes back, would you like to go with him?'

Hugh simply gazed at him, with mouth wide enough open, as Master Pennifeather would have said, to catch a cuckoo in it. 'You mean—go to Oriel?—Properly?' he stammered at last. 'Be his servitor like my father was yours—and go to lectures and things?'

'Yes,' said Mr Heritage. 'Take your time.'

Hugh looked at Martin, and Martin looked back, and they liked each other with a quick, strong liking. Then Hugh looked down at his own feet, and went on looking at them very hard indeed, without seeing them at all. It was a long time since he had really thought about going to Oxford, except in a dreamy sort of way that people think about places afar off, where they would like to go one day before they are old. But he had never quite forgotten; and now, when Mr Heritage

'What is your name?'

(See p. 207)

spoke about it, all his old longing to read books
and have his share in the New Learning flamed up
bright inside him, and he wanted most desperately
to go with Martin. And then he remembered the
Players, Jonathan more than all the rest, and he
wanted just as desperately to stay with them and
go on strolling the roads of England. Besides, they
were his friends, and he couldn't leave them just
because he had got a chance that they had not.

When you want to do two different things with
a great and terrible wanting, and you can only do
one of them, it isn't easy to make up your mind,
especially when things like loyalty come into it.
Hugh found that. On one side was his loyalty to
the Players, who had been true friends to him;
and on the other was a queer kind of loyalty to his
father, who had told him about the New Learning,
and meant him to go to Oxford. That made the
choice even harder than it would have been otherwise, and by the time he had made up his mind,
he felt as though something deep inside him had
been torn in two. But he did make it up.

'Thank you very much, sir, but—I *can't*,' he
said huskily.

'Why not, Hugh?' asked Mr Heritage.

'Well, you see, there's Argos,' said Hugh.

'Argos would come too, of course. You couldn't
take him to Oxford with you, but we would be
very kind to him while you were away, and you
would be together in the holidays.'

Hugh shook his head without a word.

'You don't want to leave the Players; that is the
real reason, isn't it?'

Hugh turned bright pink under his tan. He

would have liked to scuffle his feet, but the Players had long ago taught him not to do that.

' They're my *friends*,' he said very firmly.

' I see. You're a loyal friend, Hugh.'

Hugh turned from pink to scarlet, but he didn't say anything; and after a moment Mr Heritage laughed and got up, saying: ' I shan't take no for an answer this evening. I shall come back. By the way, how long shall you be playing in Sherborne? '

' We are starting for Shaftesbury in the morning.'

' So soon? Then I shall come back in the morning before you start out, just in case you have changed your mind. And now Martin and I will be on our way, and leave you to think it over.'

So they all went back to the inn. But there was no way out into the street excepting through the common room, and in the common room the Players had by this time gathered for their supper. There they were lounging at ease in the fire-glow with their pasties on their knees, and Argos sound asleep in their midst with his front to the leaping warmth, and several town tradesmen watching them with open mouths as though it was tremendously surprising to see Players eating like ordinary people.

They all looked up when Mr Heritage came in, and Mr Heritage turned aside to them in a friendly way; and they all swallowed their mouthfuls of pasty and got to their feet, and there were ' Good evenings ' all round. Then of course the whole story came out. Hugh had known that it would, the moment he saw that the Players were there, and his heart sank into his broken shoes. He dodged in to Jonathan's side, and stood there, utterly miserable, while Mr Heritage explained how Hugh's father had been his servitor at Oxford, and how he wanted Hugh to come and live with him and go to Oxford as servitor to his son Martin.

When he had finished, everyone began to talk at once; everyone except Hugh and Jonathan, that is. And Master Pennifeather, who was the first to get over the gasping and exclaiming stage, swept Hugh the most prodigious bow, and said: 'Did I not say you would make your fortune, if you joined our Company, my lord?'

Ben Bunsell turned to Mr Heritage and said, 'We shall be main sorry to lose him, sir, but we're all glad of his good fortune. And I'll tell you this, master, you wouldn't find a better lad to take into your house, not in all the South Country. All is not gold that glitters, *I* always say, and he certainly don't glitter much—not at present, anyways— but he's a good lad for all that.'

'I am sure you are right,' said Mr Heritage. 'The only difficulty is—that he won't come.'

Everybody stopped talking and simply stared at Mr Heritage, while Argos got up and smelled his shoes very carefully, to make sure that he was trustworthy, and then sat down and scratched behind his left ear. Usually when Argos did that people told him not to, but this time no one even noticed, and so he scratched on—and on—and on.

'Won't come?' said Master Pennifeather at last. 'Did you say "Won't *come*", sir?'

Everyone stopped staring at Mr Heritage and stared at Hugh instead, and Hugh stood with his feet planted a little apart, and his curly mouth tight shut, and stared back, as stubbornly as ever he knew how.

' I have told him not to make his choice to-night,' said Mr Heritage. ' It's difficult to decide important things in a hurry. I shall come back in the morning before you take the road.' Then he turned to Hugh and brought a hand down on his shoulder, saying, ' I hope you'll change your mind, Hugh.'

And almost before Hugh knew what was happening, he had gone, and Martin with him.

Everyone went on staring at Hugh, and Nicky let out a shrill, derisive whistle, and said, ' My eye! You don't know when you're in luck, you don't!'

But Jonathan, who had not spoken a word all the time, said, ' Don't plague him, Nicky; he's had enough,' and gave Hugh his supper, which had been keeping warm for him before the fire.

And Master Pennifeather said, ' Quite right, Johnnie. The lad's old enough to know his own mind. Therefore let us leave the subject while we enjoy these noble viands.'

So they finished their supper, talking pleasantly about the weather and the prospects of the harvest, and how well they had done in Sherborne, and things like that.

But when supper was over, Jonathan said: ' Wouldn't you like to push on to bed, now, Dusty?'

The other Players glanced at each other, and Hugh knew quite well that they wanted him out of the way so that they could talk about what had happened, without him being there to hear what they said; at least, Jonathan wanted that. So he got up and faced them all.

'I'll go to bed, but I won't go to Oxford, you know!' he said, and he stalked out with his nose in the air, across the twilit courtyard to the stable where they all slept, and kicked off his shoes and burrowed into the straw beside Argos, and lay there watching the shadows creeping in from the corners.

Quite soon Jonathan came and lit the stable lantern hanging from its beam, and sat down cross-legged to mend a torn costume, just as he had done on the first night that Hugh had spent with the Players; only this time it was his own spangled tumbler's tights, instead of the green dragon's skin. Hugh lay and watched him, and watched the lantern, and watched the gay blue flowers of his periwinkle that looked almost purple in the lantern light. And it was all so like that first night, that it made him feel quite odd, as though everything that had happened since then had been a dream.

Jonathan did not say anything until he had threaded his needle and began to sew. Then he said, more seriously than Hugh had ever heard him speak before, 'Dusty, we have been talking about what happened this evening, and I think—well, we all do, that you should go with Mr Heritage.'

But Hugh knew quite well that it was all Jonathan's idea, and that was what made it hurt. He said very firmly, 'But I don't *want* to!'

But for once Jonathan did not seem to be listening. He just went straight on talking, very quietly, but just as firmly as Hugh, pointing out the advantages of an education, and things like that. And when Hugh demanded to know who would play the girls' parts if he wasn't there, he said, 'I daresay we could find another boy, Dusty.'

At that a dreadful, aching misery swelled up suddenly in Hugh's inside, and he rolled over on to his front and said in a small, husky, furious voice, 'You want to get rid of me!'

Just for a moment nothing happened, and then, 'Don't you ever dare to say a thing like that again, Dusty,' said Jonathan's voice, with a queer, harsh sound in it.

And when he rolled over again, he saw that Jonathan had that tightened-up look that people have sometimes when they have a bad pain and are too proud to mention it.

Hugh sat up and looked at him forlornly. 'Well, then, why are you trying to make me go?—Why, Jonathan?'

'Because,' said Jonathan, 'you have been given a chance to go back to your own kind—to the sort of life and the sort of people you belong to; and people who sit down like cabbages and let their chances go by are generally sorry for it one day.'

'But you *are* the people I belong to!' protested Hugh; and when Jonathan did not answer at once, he said more loudly, 'I *do* belong to you— don't I, Jonathan?'

'No,' said Jonathan; and he began to stitch at the spangled tights again. 'Not quite—never quite, Brother Dusty-Feet.'

'But, Jonathan, I——'

'No. Listen, Dusty. You were always supposed to be going to Oxford, you know. You were on your way there when you fell in with us, because you hoped to pick up a little learning in exchange for digging people's gardens and running their errands; and now you've got a chance to go

to Oxford properly, and have your full share in the
New Learning, I think you ought to take it.'

'But I shouldn't ever see you again!'

Jonathan put in three careful stitches, then he
said: 'It wouldn't be quite as bad as that. This
isn't the first time we've played in Sherborne, and
I daresay it won't be the last.'

'You mean—you'll come back?'

'Yes, from time to time,' said Jonathan, and
looked up for an instant from his sewing. 'Dusty,
if you'll go with Mr Heritage when he comes to-
morrow, we will play in Sherborne next harvest
time. Toby will agree to that, I know.'

'You promise,' said Hugh miserably.

'Yes,' said Jonathan.

Hugh thought and thought, staring first at his
own feet, and then at Argos's ears, and then at the
bright needle flashing up and down in Jonathan's
long, brown fingers. He thought about Oxford,
and about Master Thomas Bodley's wonderful
lectures, and the glories of the New Learning that
he would be able to share, and Magdalen Tower
standing like an archangel with folded wings at
the threshold of the city. Then he thought about
the others going on without him—Jonathan going
on without him. Then he thought about Oxford
again; and he looked up slowly, and said, 'All
right—I'll go.'

And next instant, without any warning, a great
aching lump rushed up into his throat, and he said,
'Oh *Jonathan*!' and forgot about being nearly twelve.

Jonathan dropped the tights, and put a long arm
round him; and neither of them talked any more
for a bit.

XIV

THE FOOT OF THE RAINBOW

SO the next morning, while the rest of the
Company were making ready for the road,
Hugh gathered his own few belongings into a
separate bundle and put it down beside the stable
door with the pot of periwinkle, and told Argos to
guard them. Nicky had wanted him to wear the
green doublet as a parting gift, but of course he
wouldn't, so he put on the old out-grown one.
Then he went to say good-bye to Saffronilla.

Master Pennifeather had promised that they
would come back to Sherborne next harvest, and
Jonathan had made him feel much happier about
leaving the Company; but now that the time for
good-byes had really come, he was very miserable
again. Saffronilla seemed to know that he was
leaving them, and she dropped her heavy head on
his shoulder and nuzzled at him in a bothered way,
and her eyes were big and soft and troubled.

' Good-bye, Saffronilla,' he said. ' Good-bye.'

And when at last he turned away, he found that
Jonathan was standing close beside him, balancing
in his hand the lovely little dagger he always wore.

' It's all I have to give you,' said Jonathan, ' but
it's a good dagger. Pay me a farthing for it.'
(For of course you must always pay something for
a knife that is given you, or it will cut your friendship with the giver.) And he put it into Hugh's hand.

Hugh stood quite still for a moment, looking

from Jonathan to the dagger and back again. Then he turned very red, and said: 'Oh Jonathan! Oh *thank you*——' And he felt in the little pocket inside the breast of his doublet, and brought out the three-farthing bit which the old woman had given him on the very first morning of his adventures, and which he had treasured ever since.

'Here's my three-farthing bit,' he said. 'You have *that* for the dagger, Jonathan.'

So Jonathan put the tiny silver coin away inside the breast of his tattered jerkin, and Hugh stuck the lovely, keen dagger in his belt, and they stood and looked at each other.

'Oh, Jonathan, you *will* come next harvest, won't you?' said Hugh.

And Jonathan said, 'We'll come.' And then he put his hand on Hugh's shoulder and said, 'Don't you ever be forgetting this year and more that you've spent with us, nor the things you've learned in it. All your life you'll know things that respectable folk in houses can never know; and all your life you'll be one of us, because you were given Seisin of the Road. So if you come to be Lord Mayor of London or Archbishop of Canterbury, you'll still be able to claim brotherhood with every quack doctor and tumbler and Tom-o'-Bedlam who travels the roads, and it isn't many Lord Mayors or Archbishops who can say that!'

'I'll remember,' promised Hugh. 'But perhaps —perhaps I shall come back to you all, one day, when I have got my learning.'

'Perhaps you will, Dusty,' said Jonathan. 'But whether you do or not, we'll be meeting again from time to time, you and I.'

And at that moment they heard Mr Heritage's voice in the yard; so they went out to meet him. And as soon as he saw them, Mr Heritage said: ' So you're coming with me, Hugh.'

Hugh said, ' Yes, sir,' rather gruffly.

And then everybody was crowding round him, and Master Pennifeather clasped him to his chest (people did that sort of thing in those days). So did Jasper Nye and Ben Bunsell; and Nicky grabbed both his hands and pumped them up and down, saying: ' Good-bye, old lad. Look out for us next harvest.'

But Jonathan only touched him on the shoulder, and said: ' God speed you, Brother Dusty-Feet.'

Then Mr Heritage was shaking hands all round, while Hugh gathered up his little bundle and his pot of periwinkle.

' Come along,' said Mr Heritage. ' I came on foot, so there are no horses to bother about. Give me the bundle, and you can keep the pot; that's fair division of labour. Now, best foot forward.'

It was all over so quickly that Hugh really had no time to feel dreadful, and almost before he knew what was happening he was following Mr Heritage down the crooked street, with Argos padding beside him, and the soft wetness of summer rain blowing in their faces, for it was not a very nice morning.

Argos kept on looking back and whining in a troubled sort of way; and just once, Hugh looked back too. All the Players were gathered in the inn archway; Master Pennifeather with a crimson carnation behind his ear, and Jasper Nye with provincial roses on his worn-out shoes. Ben with the broken peacock's feather dangling from his hat, and Nicky in the flame-green doublet—and Jonathan, who had not even got his little bright dagger now, but still looked like Rahere the King's Jester. They waved to him, and he waved back; and then he walked straight on after Mr Heritage.

Mr Heritage began to talk at once, and went on talking so hard that Hugh was too busy listening and answering to have any time to think about having just said good-bye to his friends. He asked Hugh how old he was, and when Hugh said he would be twelve next week, he said he thought the best thing would be for Hugh to stay at home that autumn, and just get used to them all and grow a few months older, and go to the Vicar for tutoring every morning so as to catch up on his lessons, and then go to Oriel with Martin after the Christmas holidays. Then he began to tell Hugh about his father, all kinds of funny stories about the things they had done together, and how nobly Hugh's father had stood by his friend and remembered to feed him every time he got locked up in Bocardo.

So they walked on, out of Sherborne and down the muddy Shaftesbury road, between hedges gay with honeysuckle and meadowsweet, and cornfields golden-ripe for the harvest. Mr Heritage, with his feathered bonnet on the back of his head and the little bundle in one hand, talking very fast indeed over his shoulder to Hugh. Hugh marching with his legs straight and his shoulders back as the Players had taught him, and the gay pot of periwinkle in the crook of his arm. Argos stalking like a stately black-and-amber shadow at Hugh's heels.

After a bit the soft rain stopped, and stray blurs

of golden sunshine began to spread through the grey. And at last Hugh saw the roofs of a village in the distance, a nice sheltering huddle of roofs, with a church tower rising in their midst. But before they reached the village the road turned a sudden corner, and there, just in front of them, was a house; not withdrawn into its own gardens, as big houses usually are, but sitting close beside the road in the friendliest way, as though it liked to see everything that went on.

'Look,' said Mr Heritage. 'We're home.'

And Hugh looked.

The house was golden, like the Abbey and the Sun Inn; even the wavering, dipping roofs that showed above medlar and mulberry trees were golden too. But Hugh did not notice that; he was too busy looking at The Window. The friendly house had poked out a long central wing right to the edge of the road, so as to be quite sure that it really *did* see all that went on; and there, alone in the blank gable-wall, hanging out over the road like a lantern, like a jewel, like a flower, was a great oriel window. It seemed made to hold yellow candle-light after dark, as though it really was a lantern that the house had hung out to welcome home the people who belonged to it. There was no candle-light there now, of course, in the broad daylight; but instead there was the gold of late summer flowers massed in a great jar, yellow hollyhocks and marigolds and good-bye-summer.

'Oh!' said Hugh, stopping short in his tracks. 'Oh, it's lovely!'

'My lines have fallen unto me in pleasant places,' said Mr Heritage in a quiet, very contented voice.

' You are going to be happy here with all of us, Hugh.'

They turned in between mossy stone gate posts beside the gable wall, and Hugh just had time to catch a glimpse of green turf and contented flowers that looked as though they were allowed to grow as they liked best, without being interfered with, before Mr Heritage lifted up his voice in a joyous shout.

' Oie!   I've brought him!'

Next instant the starry little girl came bundling out over the low sill of an open window, picked herself out of a flower-bed with a flurry of russet skirts, and flew across the lawn to meet them. And Martin appeared round the corner of the house, with an old lean greyhound and a fubsy round-about spaniel puppy at his heels. But the starry little girl arrived first, with her skirts kilted high, and her hair bursting out in all directions from under her little lawn coif.

' Good!' said the little girl, dropping her father a respectful but hurried curtsey, and beaming joyously at Hugh.

Mr Heritage said, ' This is Antigone—Tiggy for short,' and the little girl beamed more joyously than ever.

Then Martin came up, and the greyhound and Argos began to talk to each other, blowing their cheeks in and out and giving little watchful flicks to their tails, while the spaniel pup rushed round and round them, squeaking excitedly. And somehow they all closed round Hugh and drew him with them into the big, shadowy hall of the friendly house, without his quite knowing how it happened.

He felt breathless and bewildered; but then an inner door opened, and the lady he had seen before appeared.

She came down the hall to where Hugh stood uncertainly in the middle of the family. She came rather slowly, because there was a small, round girl-child, who had only reached the staggering stage in learning to walk, clinging on to her skirts; but when she got there she smiled at Hugh in a way that took away his bewilderment and made him feel warm and wanted.

'We're so glad you've come, Hugh,' she said. 'We were afraid you would not; and we wanted you.'

Hugh found he had been quite right in thinking that she would smell nice. She did. Not of clove carnations, but of lemon verbena, which was just as good. So he smiled back at her, shyly and gratefully, although he couldn't think of anything to say.

Then the starry little girl poked a finger at the small, round one, and said, 'That's Meg. She's my sister, and she swallowed a caterpillar this morning. It was woolly.'

There was a shocked uproar at that (at least, some of it was shocked, but some of it was made by Martin trying to smother a laugh and getting it up the back of his nose by mistake). When it died down again, and Meg's father and mother had told her what they thought of people who swallowed caterpillars, which she did not seem to mind at all, Mr Heritage said, 'Martin, take Hugh off with you and show him his cubby-hole.'

And Mistress Heritage said: '*No*, Tiggy, you

can't go with them. You haven't finished sewing your seam yet.'

So Hugh and Martin went off together, up a wide, shallow staircase with a deep design of honeysuckle carved on its newel post, to a long, tapestry-hung gallery that had the lovely window at its far end. Hugh recognized it by the gleam of the golden flowers on its sill, although it looked different from the inside, as windows do. They passed through so many rooms before they got to where they were going, that Hugh wondered how he would ever learn his way about, for the old house was like a honey-comb and had no passages.

But at last they arrived in a little white-washed room with green rushes on the floor, and a truckle bed and a big polished clothes-chest, a medlar-tree peering in at the window, and a great many hawk-leashes and pots of glue, bits of wood and odd lengths of cord and sticky messes in chipped jars scattered over everything.

' This is mine,' said Martin, and pushed open one more door. ' And here's your cubby-hole.'

Hugh's cubby-hole was even smaller than Martin's, and not yet so untidy, but otherwise it was exactly the same, even to the medlar-tree peering in at the window. It was a nice cubby-hole, and Hugh liked it at once.

' Dump your bundle on the chest there,' said Martin; and Hugh dumped his bundle, and arranged his pot of periwinkle carefully in the middle of the window-sill.

Then they went back to Martin's room, because his window-sill was wider for sitting on, and sat on it and looked at each other, while Argos and the greyhound, who had come up with them, sat down on the rush-strewn floor and thumped their tails and watched. Both boys felt that they were strangers, and all at once Hugh was so desperately shy of the dark boy that his mouth went quite dry inside.

'I say,' said Martin suddenly. 'Will you tell me about being a Player?—I mean, not now—I don't expect you want to talk about it just yet; but later on. It must have been fun!'

And Hugh said, 'It *was* fun! Oh, it was! Of course I'll tell you about it, if you'll tell me about Oxford.'

'It's a bargain,' said Martin.

They struck hands solemnly, and after that, somehow they did not feel nearly so strange to each other. They sat talking in a friendly and companionable way, Hugh rubbing Argos under the chin and Martin pulling gently at the old greyhound's ears, until the door opened, and Antigone appeared.

'I've sewed my seam, and I've practised my piece, and now I've come to talk to you,' she said; and she scrambled on to the clothes-chest and sat there drumming her heels joyfully against its side.

Martin sniffed. 'That's very gracious of you, I'm sure, Tiggy.'

Hugh smiled rather shyly at the little girl, and the little girl smiled back, not at all shyly, at Hugh.

'I wanted to watch for you out of the big window, so's I could see at once if you came with Father,' she told him. 'But my Mammy said, "No!" She said, "How would you like to be watched

through windows as if you were a performing bear?"
Boy, should you like to be a performing bear?'

Hugh remembered a bear he had met at Tun-
bridge, whose bear-ward was not kind to him and
had let him get sore places on his back, and he
said, No, he didn't think he would.

'*I* should like to be a performing bear,' said
Tiggy firmly. 'I shouldn't have to sew my seam
or eat up my nice supper bread-and-milk or wash
my ears.' And she reached for a fishing-rod that
was propped in the corner beside her.

'Here, you leave that alone, Madame Meddle-
some!' said Martin. 'Or you'll go straight back
on to bread and water and *three* beatings next
Sunday!'

Just for a moment Hugh was rather startled, and
then he realized that it was a joke; one of those
private jokes that families have among themselves.
He and his father had had them, but that was so
long ago that he had forgotten until this moment.
It felt rather nice, being let into this one.

'Yes, it's very dreadful,' said Martin, wagging
his head. 'If you're going to be one of us, you'll
have to know about it. We keep her locked up in
the disused orangery and feed her on bread and
water and beat her every day—twice on Sundays.
Put that rod back, Tiggy.'

Tiggy was just stacking the fishing-rod carefully
back into its corner, with her little pink tongue
sticking out of the side of her mouth to help her
get it arranged exactly right, when in at the open
window stole a far-off swirl of music, very faint, but
very gay—and growing louder. Everybody turned
their heads to listen, as it drew nearer and nearer

yet, until they could hear the joyous lilt of drum and sackbut playing ' Mary Ambree '.

' It's our Company,' cried Hugh. ' It's Jonathan and all the rest.'

' I say, we could see them pass from the gallery window,' said Martin.

But Hugh shook his head. ' No. You go. I—I'll stay here."

So he stayed, sitting quite still in the window recess, and Martin stayed too, and Tiggy went flying off on her own to watch the Players pass.

Nearer and nearer came the music, swelling louder and more joyous every moment, and through the music Hugh could hear the clip-clop of Saffronilla's hooves and the trundling and lurching of the tilt-cart. Right along the foot of the garden it went, the little cavalcade hidden from sight by the high garden wall and the branches of the medlar tree; and then the music began to grow fainter again, as the Company went swinging on down the dusty road towards Shaftesbury. Fainter and fainter yet, until the last distant lilt of it died away into the sleepy stillness of the summer noon-tide.

' Do you—do they play tunes to march to, all the time ? ' asked Martin.

Hugh shook his head again. ' Oh no; only when we're going through a town, to make people take notice, you know. They were playing just now for a sort of—good-bye and good luck and—and don't forget us.'

Martin got up off the window-sill and said rather gruffly, ' I say, come and see my hawk. I trained her myself, and she's a beauty. You can have a

half share in her until you have one of your
own.'

But at the head of the stairs they met Tiggy.
'The Players were lovely,' said Tiggy. 'And look!
There's a rainbow with its foot in our orchard!'

The sun had begun to come out while the Players
were passing, and when the two boys looked over
her head through the great stairway window, they
saw that all the world was sparkling gold, and there
really was a rainbow—a most lovely and glorious
rainbow—with one end lost among the wooded
hills, and the other coming down into the orchard,
just beyond the herb-garden wall, so that it looked
like an orchard in a fairy-tale, where all the apple-
trees were flushed with emerald and blue and
vermilion, and the fruit shone like gems.

'Let's go there!' gabbled Tiggy. 'Let's—go—
there—at—once—this—moment!'

Somehow they all wanted to get to the foot of
that rainbow quickly, quickly, before it faded. So
they all went scurrying down the stairs, down and
down and round and round, at top speed. Half-
way down they met Meg coming up on all fours to
join them. They said, 'Hullo, Meg!' and swarmed
round and over her, and dashed on, down the stairs
and out by a side door, while Meg, who was a
persevering sort of person, turned round and
followed still on all fours, and head first, in a way
that her mother would not have liked to see.

Outside in the garden, where mint and marjoram and cinnamon roses grew all mixed up
together, Tiggy butted in between the two boys
and pushed one hand into Martin's and the other
into Hugh's, and they scurried on together, breath-

'Good-bye'

(See p. 227)

less and laughing, with the dogs dancing and yelping round them; down through the tall herbs and the rose-bushes, and out through a small fortress-looking door into the orchard beyond.

Of course the rainbow had moved on by the time they got there. They had not really expected that it would wait for them; rainbows never do. But the gold that lives at the Foot of the Rainbow was there; apples turning gold on the dripping branches of the old trees, and a golden tide of dandelions in the long grass, and a swarm of tiny, bright-eyed golden ducklings scattering and exploring everywhere, despite all that their anxious hen-mother could do to keep them together.

' Boy,' said Tiggy, after they had got their breath back, ' doesn't it feel nice, having a home of your own and a family of your own, when you haven't had one for such a long while? '

And Martin said, ' Give him time, Tiggy! He doesn't know yet.'

Now, at that moment Argos met a bright-eyed duckling round a clump of dandelions. Argos blew at it in a friendly way, and the duckling was so surprised that first it fell down flat, and then it got up and rushed squeaking to its hen-mother. But this time nobody was at all put out. Nobody but the duckling and the hen and Argos, that is. Argos had hurt feelings and his tail trembled forlornly downwards, and when Tiggy saw what was happening to Argos's tail, she sat down on her heels in front of him and put her arms round his neck, and said, ' Never mind, dearie; it just didn't understand.'

And suddenly Hugh felt quite different about

everything. He knew that it wasn't going to be easy to learn to be respectable again, after being a rogue and a vagabond so long, and he knew that he would hate wearing a clean ruff and sleeping in the same place more than four nights running. But he knew, too, that he would manage it in time, and that one day the brown man and the lady who smelled nice, the starry little girl and small Meg whom he could see in the distance arriving as fast as her hands and feet would carry her, and Martin most of all, really would come to belong to him and he to them, in the way that families do belong to each other.

So he said, 'Yes, I *do* know; and it does feel nice!'

And it did.